CAUGHT IN *a* G's WEB

Chanelle Simeon

Caught In a G's Web

Publisher Chanelle Simeon
United Kingdom

ISBN 978-1-9162370-0-1

Cover and design by Shashika Idushan

Printed in the United Kingdom

For information regarding special discounts for bulk purchases, please contact chanellesimeon@me.com

Chanelle Simeon

CAUGHT IN *a* G's WEB

Chanelle SIMEON publisher

This is a work of fiction inspired
by a few true events.
Names, characters, businesses, places,
events, locales, and incidents are either
the product of the author's imagination or
used in a fictitious manner.

Any resemblance to actual persons,
living or dead, or actual events is purely
coincidental.

ACKNOWLEDGEMENTS

I would like to thank all the wonderful people, family and friends who have supported me on this journey, you all know who you are, so a massive thank you.

To all the people who dedicated their time and efforts into helping create this book, and to all the organisations that allowed me to put them at the back of my book to try and help influence our youth to stay clear of violence, thank you.

To my three beautiful daughters, thank you for allowing me the time and space to write this book. I love you all endlessly.

CONTENTS

Chapter One

WHY?

Why? Why me? Why didn't I listen? If only I had listened. After everything, and I mean everything, this is what it had come to. Gone were the days I would proudly say I'm Darnel's girl. Why? Oh, why did I seriously not just listen? So many times I had been warned, so many times I had questioned myself, now look where I was, in some bloody alleyway in Crouch End, scared for our lives. If only I hadn't recognised that high-pitch girly voice; if only I could turn back the hands of time to six months before, my choices could have been different. Oh, how I was longing to be back in the comfort of my home right now, I can't even begin to explain.

My family, my dad, how would they all cope? The samurai sword still glistening, held high above his head was so menacing, tormenting me; it was forcing my body to hyperventilate differently. I swear, it wasn't meant to go this way. I knew he was faced with the difficult choice of having to choose between me and his childhood friend, but how many times had I done as he asked, how many times had I taken numerous risks for him and put up with his disrespect involving different girls? AND ALL FOR WHAT, was the million-dollar question, why did he call me here?

Months earlier in the summer of 1998, before I had met Darnel, I had been a normal teenager. I had good friends, a decent family and dreams of becoming an air-hostess. My mum even hired a tutor to try and help me improve my grades. I would feel like a total bitch towards my mummy who was paying huge fees to try and better my education, but I was only interested in gossip, the latest fashion and who was dating who. If only I could go back to those days, but instead, stupidly, I couldn't wait for the tutor to leave without learning hardly anything.

Like lots of teenagers my age, well, maybe most teenagers my age, I struggled with my weight. I was skinny, flat-chested and had no bum. Most of my friends, on the other hand, were quite the opposite. They had large bums, big breasts and huge thighs. If you had asked any of us back in those days, we would all have a moan about what we didn't like about our bodies or complained about our imperfections. Being a teenager was a stressful time.

There was this one particular time that's still so vivid in my mind. I can remember I was about 15 and it was a warm summer day. After school had finished, one of the girls within our group told us she had some boys to meet in Hackney. The five of us made our way to meet the group of young boys in some run-down estate. When we arrived, the boys were nowhere to be seen, so one of my friends had a bright idea and decided to go inside some abandoned flats nearby with every window smashed out to wait for the boys.

I asked my friends if they were serious about us waiting in some derelict-looking flats and explained to them that I didn't think it was a good idea. The weather was good so why couldn't we all just wait outside? Plus, if anything happened to any of us, the first question that would be asked was 'what were those girls, doing there?' I thought it better if we all just waited outside.

All the other girls thought it was a brilliant idea to go inside and wait, so turning on their heels, they walked towards the abandoned flats, leaving me standing there like a fool!

Within a matter of moments, the boys due to meet my friends were walking towards me, five of them in total. Amongst the group of five boys was this small, malnourished black one, aged around sixteen with acne covering his whole face. As the boys were passing me, one of them pushed the acne-faced boy towards me, laughing, and said, "there you go, have that skinny one as you're both skinny alike." The ugly boy had the cheek to say, "na, you're alright," and continued to walk past me.

I'm sure I turned colour as the blood drained from my face. I was so frigging embarrassed; I couldn't believe it. How dare he, he wasn't even good looking and he had the bloody cheek to say "na, you're alright" about me!

I stared at the backs of the boys until they disappeared inside the flats. I so wished I was a big strong girl right now, I would have knocked him out right in front of his friends to embarrass him, stupid bastard. Who did he think he was? Did he know how insecure I already was? Did he know how much I hated being this slim? Lots of girls my age were going through this phase. I wasn't the only skinny girl in this world, so why humiliate me in this way? Turning my back on the flats, I walked to the bus stop feeling devastated. I had known all my life I was a slim girl, of course I did, I wasn't daft, but for some reason, that day, it troubled me more than ever before. I couldn't get them horrible bastards sniggering about me out of my head.

Jumping on the 253 towards home, feelings of hurt and anger overwhelmed me. Sooner or later, my so-called friends would be leaving from them stupid dirty abandoned flats, would any of them even notice I was gone? Would them dickhead boys tell them they all laughed at my expense? I so dreaded going to school the next day, would the whole school be laughing at me when I got there? Would they tease me further about my weight? You know what, to hell with them all! One day, I would meet the guy of my dreams, a guy who would be rich and famous, and who would love me for me.

The next couple of months were the same. At school, people were gossiping about who was dating who, the boys in my year smoking or messing around at the back of the science block. Arranged fights happening in Wood Green after school, as this was the location that most schools ended up at. Oh, and the teachers lecturing us to buckle down as we only had seven or eight months before we would take our GCSEs.

So, when I met Darnel just after my sixteenth birthday at Turnpike Lane funfair, he was very different, to say the least. Just as the summer was ending, it came as no surprise I fell very quickly for him. Ever since the day acne face had made fun of me, it was as if I had a foolish point to prove inside my head. I'd allowed that one comment and them silly sniggers to shape my whole future. Darnel wasn't my usual type, he was tall, dark-skinned and a little chubby around the waist, but there was something about him that intrigued me.

I'd never had a proper boyfriend before and became fascinated by his interest in me. He was very mature compared to the guys my own age; he was two years older than me with a car. Now, that was a bonus. I thought all my dreams had come true at once. I immediately fell for his charm, but I sensed he had a different side to him fairly quickly.

The week after we'd met, he invited me out on a date to a Turkish restaurant in Highbury, I had never been on a proper date before and was excited as f**k.

I searched through every single item of clothing I had, desperate to make the best impression. I eventually settled on my new pair of skinny black jeans, a black and white expensive shirt and my kitten heel shoes that defo needed re-heeling, but still, I thought I looked a million dollars.

I was so nervous when he finally arrived. I had asked him to meet me around the corner from my house as I didn't want my mum looking out the window and spotting him. I already told her that I was going bowling with a few girls from my year and I wouldn't be home late.

As soon as I jumped in the car, his banter was so damn good, he complimented me on how great I looked. I was nervous, but he had a way of making me feel relaxed. It was only when we entered the restaurant that them bloody nerves got the better of me again. I had been looking forward to this date all day but now I was finally here, I just couldn't eat.

Darnel placed the menu in front of me and told me to order whatever I wanted. I was so hungry, I had purposely not eaten all day but now we were here, my stomach had let me down. I watched as every mouthful he took my belly rumbled in absolute pain, but yet I still just sat there and lied, telling him I wasn't hungry.

Besides the fact I didn't have any food, the date was lovely. You know them days or nights when you just don't want the moment to end? Well, this was one of them. Everything was perfect until the road rage incident. It started when we were sitting at the traffic lights, flirting, looking into each other's eyes and playing with each other's fingers. We didn't notice that the lights had turned to green but the car behind us did.

The honking of the horn coming from behind interrupted us, making us realise it was our turn to drive. Darnel took this as disrespect and flew straight out of the car. I looked on helplessly as he walked up to the car that was blowing the horn, dragged the poor man out in front of his pregnant wife and punched him straight in his face, leaving him splattered out cold on the floor. The wife's screams were unbelievably disturbing as she desperately tried to release her seatbelt to aid her unconscious husband.

I couldn't believe my eyes, there was no need for that. Yeah, the man had blown his horn but who wouldn't if they had been sitting at traffic lights and the person in front hadn't started to move?

Alarm bells should've started ringing, but instead, I shrugged them off. I let him drop me home, telling myself that it must have been a one-off as the honking had clearly pissed him off while we were sharing a beautiful moment. Arriving outside my house, he kissed me goodnight, the kiss was electric, so full of passion. My knees were weak, my knickers were wet. I had fallen head over heels.

As I was stepping out of the car, Darnel reached over to the glove compartment and pulled out a wad of cash and asked if I could look after it for him. What do you think I said, guys? 1 thousand percent YES!

As I said already, alarm bells should've been ringing! But guess what, folks? It was only the beginning.

Chapter Two

CAB DRIVER

It could only have been around four or five weeks after we'd met, after speaking to each other constantly, Darnel wanted me to follow him and one of his good friends, Joseph, to West London. As I wasn't doing anything, I told him I didn't mind coming. At about 7.30, the two of them came and picked me up in a cab and the three of us proceeded to make our way to their destination.

When we arrived, I was told to wait in the cab until they came back. After around 20 minutes, the two returned. As soon as the cab started moving, Darnel turned to me and said, "hold this," when I turned my head to see what he was talking about, I saw he was holding two handguns. I had never held a gun before, but I took them with no hesitation or questions and put them straight in my bag, he then also gave me a can of spray gas and £1200 in cash.

Driving along, I didn't even really feel phased at all, all that mattered was I was exactly where and with who I wanted to be. Arriving back to the area, we all noticed just a bit further ahead up, on the one-way road on the left-hand side, were a lot of police officers doing stop checks. The traffic on this particular night seemed to be really heavy and we could see black men being searched along with their cars. Before I could even think, 'please officers don't even look in our direction', I could see an officer's hand raised, gesturing for us to pull over.

In very slow motion, I remember thinking 'oh my gosh, I'm finished, how on earth could this possibly be happening? I only left my house about an hour or so ago, in my bag were two handguns, money and spray gas. Why did I agree to come on this journey? How on God's earth will I explain to my mum that her sweet, sweet innocent little girl she had raised was now, way, way in over her head? For a matter of fact, how will I explain this whole scenario to my part-time dad?'

Slowly, pulling up on the left-hand side with about thirty to forty officers around, I didn't know where to look. The cab driver was asked to step out of his vehicle, and in that very moment, every emotion whizzed around in my body; anxiety, fear, dread. 'All I could think of was, what on earth will I say? How long will I go to prison for? Will these guys tell the truth and tell the officers these guns aren't really mine? Can I just start running? Will I be on the 10 o'clock news?' But the biggest emotion convulsing through my mind, body and soul was fear. Fear of getting caught, fear of going to prison, but most of all, fear of looking into my mum's disappointed eyes and breaking her heart. Where would I start? How would I explain? No amount of saying sorry would be soothing enough for my mum, she wouldn't understand! Hell, I didn't even understand.

Looking up, I could see the cab driver felt nervous. The police were questioning him about his tax disc or something like that, but me, on the other hand, I was a total nervous wreck. In the back of my mind, I knew my life would change forever. OMG, what a complete fool I'd been, why didn't I just say no? In fact, why didn't I just stay at home?

Any minute now, an officer would ask all three of us to get out of the cab and search us like the rest of the people and vehicles I saw being searched. With these crazy wild thoughts running through my mind, I started to violently shake, I tried everything in my power to keep still but with all these emotions still convulsing through my mind and body, it was virtually impossible. Darnel turned to me and said, "keep still, I don't want to attract any more unwanted attention from the boys in blue." I began to mutter and stutter. I was trying to keep still but I was overwhelmed by fear.

Just when I thought things couldn't get any worse, Joseph, who was sitting in the front passenger's seat, whispered to me to pass him my bag. Darnel quickly butted in, asking Joseph why he wanted the bag. Joseph's reply made the hairs on the back of my neck stand up and my blood run cold, "if any of these police mother f**kers try it today, I'll shoot them."

Wait, was this bastard serious? He didn't want the bag to own up to the police if they found all these illegal things on me. Oh God, please, honestly help me. I just wanna go home. I never signed up for drugs, guns and now possibly murder, only LOVE. I instantly replied, “no way, I’m not passing you my bag.” Darnel quickly butted in and told Joseph to relax as they seemed to only want to speak to the driver.

Me, on the other hand, I still couldn’t relax, how could I? We weren’t safe yet. I still had all this stuff in my bag, stuff that I knew could and would send me to prison for a very, very long time. Sitting there trying my best to keep still felt like an eternity, how much longer would we have to wait? That thought was answered shortly afterwards by an officer who tapped on the window and said, “sorry to keep you guys, we won’t be much longer,”. Rolling down the window with my arm feeling heavier than it had ever done before, I responded, trying my best not to make eye contact, “oh ok, no problem.”

I had guilt written all over my face, I was sure if we stayed in this predicament for much longer and any of these officers looked me dead in the eye, they would know exactly what was in my bag and arrest me on the spot. Finally, after what felt like hours, the waiting was over, the cab driver jumped back in the car and we drove off. Halfway down the road when we all realised, we were definitely in the clear, my body was still struggling to calm down.

Darnel and Joseph erupted into a conversation that astounded me, they were talking about how lucky we all were because of what was still in the car. So, wait, what I had wasn't the worst of it?

I quietly whispered, "why are you talking in front of the cab driver for? He might take us back to the police." Darnel smirked, "don't be silly, this is my personal cabbie, he knows exactly what comes in and out of his car." For a second, I thought I heard him wrong, but after eavesdropping on the rest of the conversation, I realised I had heard right.

Ten minutes later with Darnel's arm still wrapped around my shoulder, Joseph turned and asked, "you know why we travel in cabs, cos of scenarios like this, you know, if any one of us had been driving, we would have all been going jail tonight!" He continued smiling like a Cheshire cat, "when you roll in cabs, police don't really suspect you, so it's much safer when you've got shit to do."

Chapter Three
AFRAID

Over the next couple of weeks, I still felt a little shaken up by my near fate with a long prison sentence, but equally, I felt a deeper connection than ever after what we'd been through together on the one-way road. So, when Darnel asked me one Friday night in front of his seven friends if I was coming to the cinema, I quickly responded, "yeah, no problem," knowing full well when I arrived home there would be hell to pay.

Sliding the phone out of my pocket, the time read 9.41pm. I was meant to be home by 10.30, at the same time the film was starting. How could I have said no with all his friends peering straight at me? How embarrassing would that have been? But to be honest, I wanted to go to the cinema as I wasn't ready to go home yet. Despite my curfew, I would have fun now and pay the price later.

Pulling up at the UCI cinema in Enfield, I could tell this was a busy night, music was thumping hard coming from different fancy parked cars. There were large groups of different girls all dressed up and boys trying to check out the girls, it all just seemed very chaotic.

"Babes, I'm just gonna run to the toilet then meet you guys at the popcorn stand," I mouthed to Darnel. "Yeah cool, hurry up, see you in a bit." Running into the toilet, I decided to call my mum to try and tell her some excuse or lie but she didn't answer. Sending my mum a text, I planned to tell her my friend's dad had taken us to the cinema and would be dropping me home later. Well, there you go, I thought. When my mum sees the missed call and text message, she would believe I was telling the truth.

Arriving at the popcorn stand, I couldn't see Darnel or any of his friends, all I could see were lots of people rushing around, trying to find out where their films were being screened. Other people were queuing for refreshments such as sweets, hot dogs and drinks. Taking my mobile out of my pocket to call Darnel, I could see someone standing directly in front of me. Looking up, I recognised it was Andrew, a strapping tall guy from around the way. He was a good few years older than me, 21 at the time, I think. "What's going on? You good, yeah?" Andrew asked, his voice stupidly deep, I thought as I answered, "yeah, I'm cool. And you?" Andrew grabbed my phone out of my hand and said, "nice phone, is this you?" as he continued to look at it admiringly.

You see, a couple of days earlier, I had gone with Darnel and Joseph to Stamford Hill. Sitting in the car waiting patiently as I was starting to often do, Darnel and Joseph came jogging back to the car with a bag full of goodies. As per usual, I didn't ask many questions, I was always left to my imagination, which wasn't any good thoughts these days. "Do you want this?" Darnel had asked me. Looking in his hand was the latest Nokia phone, a blue Banana phone to be precise. Although I wasn't a fan of trouble or violence, I couldn't lie or pretend that I didn't like these treats. "Thank you," I said, taking my new phone.

"Yeah, that's me," I replied. "How the hell did you get this? The phone only came out two weeks ago; you can't afford this phone!" He sounded amazed. Wait, was Andrew serious? How did he know how much money was in my pocket? How did he know if my mum or dad hadn't bought the phone for me? Bloody cheek. Observing Andrew closely, something told me he had no plans of returning my new phone.

Out the corner of my eye, I caught a glimpse of Darnel and his entourage walking towards the popcorn stand where Andrew and I stood. Judging by the cold twisted glaze spread across Darnel's face, I could sense he had the same thought as me about Andrew. "Yo, you ready?" Darnel shouted at me; his tone ignorant. Andrew, who didn't have a clue who I had come to the cinema with, took one look at the entourage stood closely behind him and in less than a split second, my new phone was back in my hand. "Yeah, I'm ready," I said, moving in the direction of screen four where our movie was being shown. Andrew, who looked like he'd seen eight ghosts, practically ran in the direction of the exit.

Entering screen four to watch the movie, Scream 2, there were hardly any seats available, the whole cinema had been taken over by mostly teenagers ready for a thrill. It was so full, I had to sit next to two strangers. I was fuming. Firstly, I was gonna get into trouble for being out past my curfew. Secondly, I was sat in between two couples, the couple on my left was a young Chinese couple wearing nothing but Burberry, who looked totally in love. The couple on my right, oh man, don't even get me started. You would have expected the young ones to talk throughout the movie, but they were completely hooked. The other older pair were extremely noisy, smelly and looked like they belonged on the Jeremy Kyle show.

Throughout the whole movie, I could hear people in front and behind telling the couple to shush, but despite the chatter and smell, I quite enjoyed the film! My only problem now was that I was two and a half hours late past my curfew, and not feeling so brave anymore.

As we were leaving the cinema heading towards our cars, I wanted to scream at the eight to hurry the f**k up because I was gonna be grounded for a whole month. Checking my mobile, strangely I didn't have any missed calls. Once we all reached the three cars parked side by side, everyone started talking about a big rave that was on, and who was on going. Darnel took one look at my expression and told the entourage he would meet them later as he was gonna drop me home first.

What a sweetheart, I smiled, blushing. I didn't even have to say a word, he just got me. Driving along to the big tune, Undercover Lover; secret affair by the American artist, Smooth, I couldn't help playing the scenario which took place twenty minutes earlier over and over again where all Darnel's friends wanted to go out, but he had put me first. Just imagine my eye contact had been enough for him to know I needed to get home. I must have been right to think we now had a real deep connection. How many people can know what you're thinking without any words?

Darnel's phone ringing sharply interrupted my thoughts. For Pete's sake, could people not just leave us alone for a few minutes? Someone was always calling his phone. "Hello, what did you say? I didn't hear you, na, I'm dropping my babes Vanessa home." OMG! Yes, yes, yes, my heart was screaming, this had to be our second most perfect night. "Why, what's wrong?" he asked with anticipation, turning down the music. There was a pause while he took in the information. "Ok, cool, I'm gonna come pick it up now." "Who was that?" I asked once he had hung up the phone. "It was my mum; she wants me to swing by hers to collect something urgently." "Is it going to take long? Cos, it's way late and I need to get home," I asked, trying not to sound too upset. "No, I'll be just two secs." So long for putting me first, so long for our deep connection.

I could kick myself; this love bubble was becoming short-lived. One minute he knew how to make me feel on cloud nine, and the next minute, don't ask. Why was I allowing him to have this effect on me?

Shortly before arriving at his mum's house on Pembury Road, Tottenham, we noticed a black tinted convertible Saab sports car driving rather slowly along Lordship Lane. As the car was driving at such a low speed, thinking nothing of it, Darnel decided to overtake. When our left turn approached and he didn't indicate, I just assumed he must be taking a longer way around. When he drove past the second left, I instantly knew something was wrong, way wrong.

"Why did you pass the two exits towards your mum's house?" I asked with a curious tone. "I think the black Saab behind is following us," he said calmly. The next left Darnel took, the Saab took. No, surely this couldn't be happening, "take the next right," I said with a shaky voice, sure enough, the Saab took the right. Now, let me explain, this instant fear that was ripping through me like lightning was like no other.

This wasn't like the time when Darnel, Joseph and I got pulled over by the police on the one-way road, that was scary, but this, this had reached an all-new high. This was closing my eyes for a few seconds, watching all my friends and family standing over my graveside.

This was seeing my mum age fifty years in the space of a week, for not being able to cope with the loss of her sixteen-year-old daughter. This was my little sister asking repeatedly for me and my mum having to explain to her that I had gone to heaven. This was also my dad trying to explain to my half-brother that he and I would never get the real chance to bond.

Oh, Lord, please, please I beg of you, help me.

My legs turned to jelly, the palms of my hands sweaty, my forehead, nose and back were now completely wet. My heart was beating so fast and loud, I was sure I was gonna have a heart attack.

Glancing over to Darnel, who's eyes were now fixated on the rear-view mirror, gave me no comfort at all. Although Darnel and his entourage despised the police, I was sitting on the edge of my seat, clutching the door handle as tightly as I could, twisting my neck vigorously from side to side, desperately scanning the high road to see if I could notice a police car to rescue me.

"Quick, quick, pass my phone," Darnel shouted. My mind went completely blank, where the hell was his phone? Hands trembling, I saw the Motorola mobile situated in the armrest between us. "Hurry up, quick, call David." Panting, I replied, "I dunno how to use this phone." "Pass it, pass it," he snatched the phone and was fumbling as he made the call. "David, quick, bring the ting downstairs," he commanded, slightly agitated. "David, I said bring the f**king ting downstairs and meet me in the alley near Sainsbury's now."

Was this seriously gonna be the last time we drove along Tottenham High road towards Edmonton? Was this the last time I breathed fresh air into my lungs? This fear, anxiety and stress was now so overwhelming, I didn't even notice the warm sensation of wee trickling down my black leggings.

God, I promise you I will never defy my mum again. I promise, if you let me live, I will always try my best to make it home on time for my curfew, please, Lord, I don't deserve to die.

Pulling up frantically to the near pitch-black alley, I could just about make David out. David was dressed in dark denim jeans and a dark coloured shirt which wasn't even buttoned up correctly. Black hat and gloves, he seriously looked like a max murderer, with one hand down the front of his trousers and death behind the eyes. I knew he was a young soldier who would kill or die for Darnel.

As soon as Darnel spotted David, he jumped straight out the car, "fam, pass the ting, pass the ting," I could hear Darnel ordering. Struggling to see what the ting was that he wanted to be passed, it definitely looked very similar to the small gun I had hidden for him recently.

Turning around whilst holding my breath to see if I could still spot the tinted Saab, I couldn't make out the driver for the full-beam lights were blinding. The pair now approaching the car made me squeeze my eyes tightly shut, anticipation and paralysis threatening to shut down my whole body.

Breathe, Vanessa, breathe. I had to remind myself, for I swear I was on the verge of passing out.

1...2...3...4...5...to my amazement, I hadn't heard a single sound. Forcing my eyes open, I had to blink a few times. Standing in the doorway of the Saab was a frigging girl. Can you believe this shit? It was Darnel's ex-girlfriend named Hazel! Hazel, the bitch, was dressed in a dark grey Nike tracksuit, a black Nike cap and huge gold hoop earrings.

Do you really mean to tell me that all this tremendous fear, anxiety and stress was down to this dumb Hazel chick? What was it she didn't understand? Darnel was with me now and didn't want her anymore! Hazel started to rant and rave, making a whole heap of noise, probably because she saw me, I'm not even totally sure. Now, I'm not an insensitive type of person, but Hazel, like seriously, this looks pathetic, you're 22 and he's 18, he's basically telling you to piss off and go away, but you're still pleading and begging to talk to him. WOW!

David took one look at the spectacle displayed in front of him and said, "pass the ting, fam, I ain't got time for domestics, I'm going back to my yard." My fear was beginning to turn to serious anger; why didn't Hazel just move on? Seriously, she should be dating someone her own age.

"Darnel, please, we need to talk, why you treating me like this? I love you." "Hazel," Darnel said with disgust, "stop embarrassing yourself and go home." "Darnel, please don't do this to me. If I ever meant anything to you, then please just talk to me. Please, Darnel, I beg you." She pleaded in desperation, whining on about how unfair Darnel was being. It was as if I wasn't even there, although Hazel had definitely seen me. It felt like the only person who she could see in her world was Darnel. "Hazel, low it, whose car is this anyway? Stop stalking me and my girl, and find your yard," he sounded fed up and annoyed.

Sitting there I was flabbergasted, if I hadn't witnessed and seen all this pleading and begging for myself, I would never have believed it. Driving off and looking back in the wing mirror, I felt sorry for dumb Hazel. It's funny how someone's emotions can change from fear to anger and sorrow all in a matter of minutes. That night arriving home, I made a promise to myself; I would try to never allow myself to be humiliated like Hazel.

Chapter Four

REFLECTION

On Saturday morning, I couldn't wait for my mum to hurry up, get dressed and leave. My mum had been running a Caribbean food take away cabin in Walthamstow market for the past four years. Every other week, me and my younger cousin, Stacey, took it in turns to help my mum out. This week it was Stacey's turn, leaving me all the time in the world to go to Angel to my good friend Rebecca's house.

"Mum, what time did you get in last night? I didn't even hear you come in," I asked while entering the kitchen and heading towards the fridge. "Oh, umm, I went to a party over in Hackney with Theresa," she replied, not looking up from the table.

Phew, I breathed, thank goodness we'd missed each other by a mere 35 minutes. I had heard my mum arrive home but pretended to be asleep, so happy I wouldn't be grounded for a whole month.

"How was the film you lot watched last night, any good? I saw your missed call and text but forgot to call you back," she asked, now giving me eye contact. "Yeah thanks, it was good, we watched a scary movie called Scream 2 and then Nazarene's dad dropped me home about half twelve. Mum, ain't you tired?" I asked as I poured orange juice into a glass. "It's six o'clock and still pitch-black outside," I exclaimed as I was having difficulty trying to make out the trees, it was so dark. "No, I'm fine, you know I can't afford to take the day off, my customers rely on me," she said, reaching for the TV remote. "Plus, Christmas is around the corner, how long we got again?" she asked. "Three weeks and two days," I said, rolling my eyes.

"Mum, turn on the heating please, it's freezing in here," I was sure it was colder than outside. Seriously, I could never understand why our house was so cold. "Go back to bed where it's warm, gas is too expensive," she snapped back, her hands now full of soap from washing the breakfast dishes. "Anyway, what you doing awake? It's not your turn to come market this week," she quizzed, realising the time and how strange it was that I was wide awake. "I know, I know, but I was thirsty so I came downstairs to make myself a glass of orange, and now I feel like I can't sleep." "Well, you best go back to bed cause as soon as I'm finished these dishes, I'm gonna get ready as it's nearly time for me to collect Stacey."

Jumping back into bed, I started to toss and turn. I so wanted to call Rebecca right now, but it was too early. I couldn't help my mind drifting to all the events that had unfolded last night, the episode with Andrew and my new phone, Darnel leaving the entourage to drop me home, and then, of course, the car following of looney Hazel. I wonder how she slept, if she got any sleep at all. I wonder if she'd tell her friends of her pathetic behaviour in front of me. Closing my tired eyes, I must've drifted off.

Waking up a few hours later with a startle, I was breathless, my heart was hammering, and the sheets were soaked. Scanning the room, I realised I was ok. I was home safe in bed; it had all just been a nightmare. My nightmare had been about a car chase, three masked men chasing me through the streets of London whilst I was desperately trying to get away. I crashed into a charity shop and then blacked out for a minute or so, only to find the masked men stood directly above me about to shower a round of bullets into my skinny flesh. Thank goodness this was only a dream, I thought as my heart began to return to its usual beat.

Removing my phone from under my pillow, I scrolled through my contact list, stopping at Rebecca. I dialled her in, "Hi, Becks, where are you? You at home? You're not gonna believe what happened to me last night!" "Why? What happened," Becks asked eagerly. "I'll tell you when I get there." I didn't want to tell her all over the phone. I wanted to see her expressions; you can't get that over the phone. "Nooo, tell me now," she insisted, "no I'll tell you when I get there in about two hours or so." I loved my friend Becks, short for Rebecca, I really did, she was always the one I could turn to, she always had an open ear.

Walking the six-minute journey to Manor house train station, I so needed to get myself a thicker jacket. This weather was ridiculously cold, heavy snow had fallen overnight, the wind was blowing fiercely and to top it all off, I had worn my bloody sliders, making my toes feel like ice.

I promised myself when the new year started that I was gonna find myself a part-time job and enquire about taking some driving lessons. My mind now wondered back to when looney Hazel jumped out of the car. If I was old enough to start learning to drive, then there was no way next year I weren't driving. Just imagine if it hadn't been Hazel following us, imagine it was an enemy of Darnel's, I would have had no way to escape.

Arriving at Glorious Street in Angel where Rebecca lived with her lovely foster mother, Judith, I was dying for a pee. Hopping from side to side on the doorstep while I waited for Becks to open the front door, I must have looked like a right fool to any strangers passing by. Once the door was opened, I flew straight past Becks without saying hello. She shouted out after me, "So, what happened to you last night?" I shouted back, "Wait one sec, I'm bursting for the loo." I didn't know what was going on, but recently, I was finding it hard to hold my pee.

As soon as I'd finished in the toilet, I went to find Beck's mum, Judith, to say hi, but she was out. Walking into Beck's huge bedroom on the second floor, I saw another friend of ours named Blessing sitting on the bed. Blessing was a cool African girl from school. I liked Blessing, but my only problem with her was that sometimes she could be too man hungry. Most guys who gave her the time of day got into her knickers quick and I mean, really quickly. Blessing was a girl without a whole lot of morals or self-respect, she wouldn't hesitate to lay down with your boyfriend given the chance. I found this very strange seeing as her parents were really strict and from a strong religious background.

There was this one occasion when we were all about fourteen, Blessing, Becks, me and a white boy from our school named Patrick all went to Blessing's house to do our English homework. As we entered the house, we were all just about to say hello to Blessing's dad who was halfway down the stairs, when in the thickest African accent, you will ever hear, he said, "What is this? Why are they here? Why you bring this white boy to my house?" The rest of what he said we couldn't understand as it was all said in his language. Blessing looked at us all and immediately told us we needed to leave; she never came to school for a whole week. That was the first and last time we ever went over to her house.

"Hey, Vanessa," said Blessing in a concerned tone, "what happened to you? Becks said something happened, you ok?" It was a concerned tone but patronising, like the way a teacher would be talking to a 3-year-old. Becks and her bloody big mouth, I thought, smiling at Blessing. "Yeah I'm fine, just feeling a bit tired," I answered, trying to change the subject. "So, tell us what happened to you last night?" she asked again. Both girls were eyeballing me. "Well, the thing is, so many things happened last night, I don't even know where to start," I responded, looking from left to right at them both. "Start at the beginning," Blessing said, bouncing on the bed eagerly.

"Wait, guys, first let me light up a cigarette." Ever since small acne face and his friends had made fun of my weight on that run-down estate, I had taken up casual smoking, as I said before, it troubled me differently. Becks and Blessing were both smokers a long time before me, Becks sometimes even smoked weed, but since that day, I found myself picking up the same bad cigarette habit. I only ever really smoked one or two a day, but today, I was already on my fourth.

"Right, so firstly, I saw Andrew and he snatched my phone, next..." I was interrupted by Blessing who asked, "who the hell is Andrew, and who did you go to the cinema with?" "Yeah," said Becks, slightly irritated, "you're not telling us the whole story, start back at the beginning and don't leave out any details." I took a long deep pull on my cigarette and then blew out a steady stream of smoke.

"Ok, ok, so last night Darnel asked me if I wanted to go cinema in front of all his friends, so I went, next, when we get to the cinema..." "wait," said Blessing, interrupting again, "was sexy Joseph there?" "Blessing, seriously please stop doing that, just let me finish what I'm saying and then ask your questions after, plus, anyway, I'm talking to Becks," I said rudely, slightly annoyed by her constant interruptions.

"SOOORRRRYYY, as I was saying before I was rudely interrupted," Becks let out a giggle, we all looked at each other and burst out laughing, it was so hard to stay mad at any of these two. "Now, let me finish the story," I said whilst stumping out my cigarette.

"So, do any of you two remember that guy named Andrew, from Leyton I think, he's a little bit older than us and allegedly dangerous," "does he hang around with that short light skin boy from Finsbury Park with a deformed arm?" Becks quizzed, "yeah, I think so. Member about a year ago when we all heard the stories of those two boys going around doing a smash and grab on mopeds to nuff jewellery shops in the endz? Well, anyway, I saw one of them last night at the cinema. Don't think he didn't grab my phone out of my hand like he was on a rude boy ting, when he turned his head and saw who I was with, he was over shook."

"Don't lie, did Darnel say anything to him?" "Becks, trust me, he didn't have to, Andrew was so prang, you might as well say he threw the phone back in my hand and practically ran for the exit."

"Then, to top it all off, when we had left all Darnel's friends and he was dropping me home, we were followed by a Saab with its windows fully tinted, every turn we took, the Saab took. I can't even begin to explain how my heart was thumping. I was so scared, I thought I was gonna die." "For real?" Blessing said, the first question she had asked since I'd told her not to interrupt me. "Yep, seriously," I continued, "and you lot are not gonna believe who it was following us."

Before any of them could even ask, I blurted out, "Hazel." "Hazel?" they both echoed, looking completely shocked, "yep, Hazel," I said again, this time nodding my head along in agreement. "WTF!" shouted Becks, "following you guys for what?" "Becks, if you were ever there and heard how much she was begging him to talk to her, you would have been shocked. She was begging so much, I started to feel sorry for her." "Wow," said Blessing, "I can't believe what you're telling us, did she say anything to you?" "Nope, she never said a word, she saw me, but it was as if I weren't even there."

"OMG, I swear she's like six or seven years older than us, don't she have any shame? Begging a man to talk to her and especially in front of another girl." Later to that, Becks frowned, moving her head from side to side, crossing her arms and legs in disgust at Hazel's behaviour. "Becks, that's the same thing I was thinking about all night, I was dying to phone you when I got home but it was way too late. All I know is that could never be me," I announced proudly, "me neither," chipped in Blessing.

"So, what did Darnel say to you? Did he say anything?" "The worst thing, Blessing, is that he didn't say much at all which further pissed me off. I asked him what all that was about but he just grinned and shrugged and told me Hazel was obsessed with him. I tried to continue the conversation, but he just shut me down. As I was getting out of the car, he handed me three hundred pounds and told me to buy something nice for Christmas, probably to shut me up." "Vanessa, I dunno what's up with Hazel but if I was you, I would be very careful, she doesn't seem all 100% there."

"Yeah, I hear you guys. When I next see Darnel, I'm gonna question him. If I don't like what he's telling me, then we're finished." "Yeah, yeah, you ain't going nowhere, you're way too hooked on him, plus, Vanessa, I told you already to be careful when you're with or around Darnel, he's a serious gangster." "Becks, leave him alone, he's just misunderstood, but listen, I'm not playing these silly games with him and his ex, he just better make sure he sorts all this shit out."

For the rest of the day, the three of us sat about chilling, talking and laughing. By the time I looked at Rebecca's clock situated above her double wooden bed, it was already 17:47. Where does the time go? I wondered. As I was getting up and ready to leave, something within me was telling me to stay, I can't explain why, how or what, but I just felt it.

"So," Becks said, starting up another conversation about Darnel and Hazel, "what you gonna do?" "Becks, truthfully, I'm not sure what to do, I know it's only been a couple of months for me and Darnel, but I love him," I said, sitting back down. "I know guys lie and talk rubbish, but Hazel does seem obsessed with him, that's not his fault, remember, she acted as if I wasn't there and Darnel told her to leave him and his girl alone," I reminded them, smirking. "Yeah, but," Blessing added, "think about this logically, if she's obsessed then she's not gonna leave him alone, is she?"

I paused for a second while I thought about what Blessing was saying, "well, I'm hoping that sooner rather than later she will get over him, just get on with her life." Midway through our conversation, we were all interrupted when suddenly Blessing's mobile began to ring. By the way Blessing's eyes widened, I knew whatever this call was about had shocked her to the core.

As Blessing was ending the call, which only lasted seconds, she was screaming at Becks to quickly change the channel to the news channel. The image of what we all saw, and which will stay with me forever, was of a couple we all new. The couple had been arrested the year before due to a tip-off to the police about James supplying drugs and guns to a huge selection of different people and raking in lots and lots of money. Pauline, on the other hand, didn't sell drugs or guns but had been caught up in all James' shit.

The pair had been remanded in prison since their capture last year and were awaiting sentencing. Today, James was given ten years and Pauline eight. The three of us just sat in total silence, unable to speak, our jaws hitting the floor. My shoulders slumped forward, my chest felt heavy, my eyes glistened with heavy teardrops, I felt so upset for Pauline and afraid for myself.

This shit was real, over real, this could've been me with my picture plastered all over the news. Reflection hit me like a ton of heavy bricks. My mind now racing back to the evening on the one-way road, every single emotion came flooding back doubled. How was it my oldest and dearest friend had been given such a harsh prison sentence for just falling in love? This bullshit wasn't fair, plus Pauline, who was almost three years older than me, had a two-year-old son from a previous relationship, who was gonna look after him?

Picturing Sam, Pauline's 58-year-old mother, who I'd known since I was a little girl, my heart broke, shattering into a million pieces. Pauline and I had been best friends ever since I can remember, she was like the big sister I never had. Our families knew each other as well as we only lived two roads away from each other.

Pauline was one of five children; her father had tragically died in a road traffic accident some many years back when she was ten. All the rest of the siblings were males and much older than she was. Pauline's mother, Sam, was a real good woman, she worked hard all her life and made sure her kids never went without. In some ways, she really did remind me of my mum. Just 18 months ago, she had been diagnosed with terminal lung cancer.

Around this time, Pauline and I fell out, it must have been over something so trivial cos I can't even remember what it was. Being two of a kind, stubborn, and hard-headed, we hadn't made up. I'd just assumed we'd make up one day in the near future. I so wanted to embrace my oldest and dearest friend and tell her everything was gonna be alright. Only God knows how I missed her. Although I was still sitting amongst Becks and Blessing, I had never felt so alone.

I knew then and there why I'd had that sixth sense, a strong feeling to stay a little longer at Beck's house. I wasn't meant to miss the news, that subliminal message I believe was a way of letting me know I was getting too caught up. It was now time to reflect on my own life, but did I listen?

Chapter Five

SCHOOL GATE

The first day back to school after what had happened to Pauline, I still felt annoyed and upset about the whole weekend. It didn't help looking out the window and seeing nothing but pure darkness and thick fog. This was meant to be a happy time for me, this was my last ever Christmas at school, plus, I couldn't shake off this constant unwell feeling. I just wanted to jump back into bed and bury my head under the pillow.

Frigging hell, this house was cold. Getting ready for school was like torture, the freezing tiles in the bathroom beneath my feet were turning my body numb. My body felt sluggish, my head was pounding, my energy felt drained and believe it when I say, it didn't help to find out there was no gas. Great, could this day get any worse?

Boiling the kettle several times to make myself a small bath, I began daydreaming about what today would unfold. By now, I knew everyone had seen the news on TV and if you missed it, you were sure to get a phone call about it, enabling you to watch the repeat. Everybody at school would be talking or whispering about it, making out like Pauline deserved what she got. I knew Pauline personally; she was like my big sister before we fell out and she didn't deserve the heavy sentence she got but trying to convince some people otherwise would be a very hard task.

Sighing heavily, I reminded myself this didn't bear thinking about right now, the most important thing was contacting Sam, Pauline's mum, to see how she and little man were doing.

Entering the school gates that morning 10 minutes before the bell rang, I braced myself for all the nasty and sly comments I expected to hear, but to my surprise, most people were full of empathy and sorrow for Pauline.

There was this one bitch named Patsy Dudd, who was in the year below us, chatting rubbish at lunchtime, but then again, she always talked rubbish. Patsy was a short bow-legged girl who believed that because she was light skin with soft wavy hair, she was nicer looking than everybody else.

Walking into the lunch hall, I overheard bow-legs talking shit as per usual, telling people how Pauline deserved what she got and that she hoped social services took away her son. When I heard this, I flipped, I grabbed the nearest thing to me which was a lunch tray and battered that chubby bow-legged bitch. By the time I finished with her, her lip and nose were bleeding. I made sure she apologised loudly in front of the whole lunch hall.

I felt elated straight after the fight, I had everybody coming up to me asking what had happened, how she must have upset me because I wasn't into fighting or known for fighting at all. When I explained to them that I'd overheard her saying how she hoped social services took away Pauline's son, they all agreed she'd gone too far this time, and that beating was a long time coming for all the mix up she had caused in the past.

Amongst the crowd questioning what had happened was a nice white girl named Sarah. Sarah whispered in my ear that she didn't want to get involved or cause any trouble, but she had just come out of the math's block toilets where Patsy and her friends were. She said she overheard Patsy phoning her older twin brothers, Ben and Stan, to come and beat me up after school, telling them I'd humiliated her by making her apologise in front of everybody at school.

Ben and Stan were known as 2 old school Gs, I wouldn't stand a chance with these two grown arse men. By now, I was strongly regretting my decision to batter Patsy. Why the hell did I make myself come to school? I sensed from this morning this day wasn't gonna be a good one. I should've just told my mum I needed to stay home.

"Who gives a shit?" I mouthed off to Sarah in front of the group of girls stood all around me, trying my best to make out like I wasn't bothered when, truthfully, inside I was petrified. All I wanted to do right now was run. What would they do? Punch me, slap me, spit on me? Forget this shit, the uncertainty was killing me. I so wanted to call Darnel, but I had to first think about all my options here. Perhaps I was stronger than I looked, maybe I could fight them both, but how? They were grown, arse men. Tell one of the teachers? Nope, that was out of the question, or apologise in front of the whole school? But I'd done nothing wrong. I was left with no options here, Darnel it would have to be.

Calling Darnel, the first time with no response, I began to panic. I started to convince myself the twins weren't gonna wait until after school, they were on their way to beat me up right now. Darnel answered his phone on my second attempt, I was talking so fast he didn't hear a word I said. "Vanessa, slow down, man, slow down, I can't hear what you're saying, what's wrong with you?" "I just had a fight with some bitch called Patsy cos, remember my old friend who got sentenced on the weekend I was telling you about? Well,"

"Vanessa Fox," I heard in a loud and authoritative tone, "put that phone down at once." I froze, I didn't know what to do, I so needed to continue this conversation with Darnel, but Mr Brown, our head teacher, had caught me red-handed. I could hear Darnel calling my name over and over again, but Mr Brown's angry face and stern stance made me hang up.

"Pass me your phone at once, I'm confiscating this till the end of the day. You're very lucky indeed we're breaking up for our Christmas break this

Friday, or I would've held on to your phone for two weeks. I'll be sending a letter home to your mum explaining why you have an hour's detention on Thursday. How many times do I have to remind you kids you're not allowed mobile phones on school premises? You should be setting a good example to the younger children."

I wanted to relieve myself of this heavy burden by telling Mr Brown that Patsy's older twin brothers were coming to mash me up after school. Explain to him in detail how deeply afraid I was, and that I needed to call Darnel to come and protect me because I had no other alternatives. With my head down looking at the ground, all that came out of my mouth was, "sorry, Mr Brown."

"Collect your phone from the office at the end of school, and once again, let me make myself very clear, mobile phones are not permitted anywhere on our school premises. If you're caught again, I will have no choice but to suspend you." "Yes, Mr Brown," I responded, still staring at the ground.

"Now, go on, make your way to your next lesson, the bell's about to ring." "Yes, Sir." Doubling back on myself, I made my way through the big brown corridors and up the steep steps that led me to my next lesson which was double math's. Just as I was arriving in the classroom, I spotted Blessing. Clapping eyes on her, I felt like I'd won the lottery.

"Blessing, quick, I need to use your phone," I asked, sighing with relief, "what's going on? I've just come back from the chicken shop on the high road, and it's all over the school that you had a fight with bow-legs, and apparently her twin brothers are coming down after school for you."

"I know, I heard her brothers are coming down for me, that's why I need your phone, Mr Brown caught me and confiscated my phone just as I started speaking to Darnel," "But, Vanessa," she exclaimed, "I've just used all my credit, so what are you going to do now?" she asked, looking sympathetic and concerned.

My eyes flew open like saucers, I didn't know whether to laugh or cry, I was becoming fed up with this, how many times in recent weeks had I found myself plagued by fear? I had found myself in an impossible situation. I only had two hours before I was made into a punching bag by two grown arse men in front of the whole school. Sitting down at my table at the back of the class, I couldn't concentrate at all. If only I could get a message to Darnel then I would be ok, but how? Hardly anybody in my class had mobile phones and the ones that did never had any credit.

Usually in life, when someone's afraid of something, minutes feel like hours, but at this point in time, the minutes seemed to disappear into seconds way too fast for my liking. Every second was getting too close to my nearing fatality. By the time the bell had rung for the end of the day, I had only written my name on the top of the mock exam sheet.

Walking with Blessing and Becks to the office to collect my phone, it was written over both girl's faces I was completely on my own once we reached those school gates. I couldn't blame them though; they were scared just like me. The closer we got, my steps resembled those of a pigeon, my legs felt like thick wood, my stomach ached, and I could feel the vomit forming in my throat.

In the near distance, a crowd had begun to form. Scanning the crowd, I spotted Patsy standing right at the front, her eyes confidently on me. I tried my best to show no fear, still, I continued to walk, what choice was there now? Only ten feet separating us, the crowd stepped back to give us just enough room for the fight. I firmed my body the best way I knew how and braced myself, dropping my head to look at the ground, hoping by some miracle the floor would open up and swallow me whole.

"Yo, babes," my head flew up, my eyes dashed around, was my mind playing tricks on me? I thought I'd heard the familiar voice I was longing to hear. Making his way through the crowd was my Mr Handsome. The relief I felt, I can't even explain, it was just indescribable. "Yo, dickheads, don't let me ever hear you made this mistake again, about you're coming for my gal, furthermore, pass me your car keys," Patsy looked traumatised, she didn't know where to look, she'd called her brothers for me but now the tables had turned and they were getting roughed up, she had made the wrong move. I couldn't help but smirk at her.

The twins tried their best to talk their way out of it, explaining they had only come to chat to me, but Darnel was having none of it, threatening to put both twins inside his boot. The twins handed over their Astra car key which he put straight in my hand. I didn't even know how to drive, but I assumed it was just to take the piss. As we walked towards his car, I could hear the gasps of shock. I asked him how he knew I was in trouble, and he said, "don't worry, babes, I've told you already I've got you." If I thought I loved him before, I truly loved him now.

Chapter Six

HEART BROKEN

It was two days before Christmas, and I had hardly spoken to Darnel. Since the incident with the twins, I had fallen deeper than ever in love with him, but he seemed to become quite distant, which I couldn't understand because I thought we had something special. It was only last week he rescued me from them, twins. Recently, I would call his phone and hear another girl talking in the background. When I would inquire who he was with, he would ignore me and continue talking about something else, or mention the fact that he might need me to do something for him. I would convince myself he must be with one of his friends, and it was probably one of their girlfriends, but deep down, I knew the truth, I just didn't want to admit it to myself as I was now becoming more like dumb Hazel.

To hell with Darnel. If he wanted to fool around with other girls, then he could, but I wasn't gonna stay around. What I needed to do now was focus on myself, Sam, Pauline's mum, and find out how little man was doing. When I arrived at Sam's house later that day, I was shocked to the core when I saw the size of her tiny frame, her ribs were sticking out from behind her slim-fit floral shirt. The white tracksuit bottoms swung around her bony hips, her scalp was bald, and her posture was now completely bent.

"Hi, Vanessa, come in, come in," Sam urged with a weak voice, holding onto the wall for support while walking slowly in extreme discomfort. I wanted to instantly cry but fought back my bitter tears. "Hi, Sam, how are you?" I asked with a broken heart. "Not very well, honey. I am very weak, but still thanking God for each day he allows me to open my eyes." Walking slowly behind Sam entering the front room, it still looked and smelt the same, the fireplace looked as magnificent as ever with all the family photos still decorating it beautifully, apart from the boxes of toys stacked in the corner and a bed now where the sofa used to be, it really did have the same warm feeling as ever.

So many beautiful memories I had in this house, like the time when I was about 9 and Rebecca 12 and we baked biscuits together with her mum, but they had all burnt, so we all fell about laughing and started all over again. Another time, we were sent to bed about 10 pm, but we thought it was too early and spent the whole night talking quietly, hoping we wouldn't get caught.

"Sam, is there anything I can get you? Or is there anything you need?" "No, honey, I'm fine, just very tired all the time." "I've come to see how you're all doing, have you spoken to Pauline? How's she coping and how's the little man doing?" Sam looked like she was starting to go in and out of consciousness, I could tell she was far worse than I ever imagined. Sam tried to answer the questions I had just asked her but started coughing chronically. "It's ok," I tried to reassure her, helping her to lay slightly back while wiping the bit of blood now starting to spill from her mouth.

Grabbing the box of tissue near the foot of the bed, I helped Sam softly wipe away the blood. "Sam, it's ok, I'm sorry if I asked you too many questions at once, just try to rest." "Can you pass me a glass of water please?" Sam asked. She then sipped the water I brought her and cleared her throat, "You know, Vanessa," Sam said, gazing through a small gap in the curtains, "I pray to God every day my girl is ok! I have spoken to her a few times and she seems to be alright, but I'm too weak to go and visit her. Adam, who's now two and a half, has gone to live with his other grandmother as I can no longer take care of him."

Teardrops rolled down her face while she continued to gaze, wiping away her tears with the back of her hand, she started to sit up, looking a little bit more energised than when I had first arrived. Changing the subject, Sam said, "enough of being sad, how are you and the family doing? Make sure you continue to grow into the beautiful young lady you are." I smiled. This was typical of Sam even though she was not far from death's door, she was always still thinking about others.

"Are you sure I can't get you anything?" I asked again. Wanting by some miracle to see the same old full of life chubby mummy I used to see, "no, honey, the palliative team come and look after me three times a day." "Who are the palliative team?" I asked naively. "They are a team of nurses who look after you when you're near the end of your life, they feed me and make sure I take all my painkillers and medicines." Sam must have seen the heartbreak in my face because she said, "honey, I don't want you to worry about me."

"Vanessa, I've seen you grow up from a little girl and I love you like you're my own, I just want you to do well at school and get a good job. My Pauline is a good girl as well, you know that, she just made some bad choices with the boys that she liked, and I want you two to make up. Promise me you two will sort out your differences, cos as you can see, life is too short." I nodded to show Sam I fully understood what she was saying.

I stayed with Sam the whole day that day, hoping this wouldn't be the last time I saw her. Each time Sam fell asleep, silent tears would roll down my face, not wanting to be seen crying. I watched the lovely nurses from the palliative team try their best to make Sam as comfortable as they could, but when I could see the pain becoming overbearing, I held her hand tight, letting her know I was there for her.

After all the soaps had finished that evening, it was finally time for me to go home. I was knackered, so I said goodbye, kissing Sam on the forehead and promised I would be round to visit again soon. Closing the front door behind me, I couldn't hold back the overflow of tears dying to spill from my eyes. I felt so disappointed with myself. Pauline and Sam both needed me, but I had been stubborn and selfish. I had known for a long time about Sam's Cancer but had only gone around when it was now, practically too late.

Deep in my feelings, while walking to the bus stop, Darnel called me saying he wanted to see me. I was feeling quite low and just wanted a hug, plus it wasn't too late so I could quickly go and see him and then make my way home. When I got to his friend's house in Walthamstow, where he had asked me to meet him, I was shocked to see bare goons stood outside the house, all looking like someone had died.

When Darnel saw me walking towards the door, he walked out, coming to meet me slightly away from the crowd. "Vanessa, babes, I need you to do something for me, some madness has happened today, and I need you to take this money and food (drugs)." I looked at him, devastated, did he know what type of day I'd had today? Couldn't he tell I felt so deflated? I thought, somehow, he knew I was really sad and needed a big hug.

"Some dickheads ran up on my bredrin, Plastic, earlier today and stabbed him up. I've just come from the hospital where he's fighting for his life, but there are too many feds up there." "Really?" I said, surprised, looking around a bit scared, not wanting to be caught in any drive-by. "Yeah, they see him and my next bredrin, Slimzy, walking and jumped out on them. Slimzy managed to get away, but Plastic is in a f**king bad way, dem pricks have to pay, on my mother's life they have to pay."

I stood there completely silent, not wanting to say the wrong thing, eyeballing the crowd and then Darnel. The tension in the atmosphere felt like it could cut the air. The aroma of weed coming from his friends was strong, every single one of them dressed in dark clothing and looked pissed as hell. For the second time in a day, I was deep in my thoughts, I wanted to tell him to leave it alone, but I could see they were all ready to roll. "I'm so pissed," he continued, "do them man dere really think they can f**k with my soldiers? Listen, the money and food are in my glove compartment, take it with you just in case". "Just in case of what?" I began to ask, "Just in case, take the stuff with you and if need be, then take it to my mums' tomorrow."

"Darnel, we're ready to move, just say the word," one of his soldiers called out. Walking away from the group and making my way home, I fretted non-stop, what if Darnel and his friends' plan backfired and he got seriously injured? What if he seriously injured someone else, could I be with a man who had killed another human being in cold blood? Or what if he got caught carrying a weapon by the police and was sent to jail? That night, arriving home, I made my excuses and went straight to bed but didn't sleep a wink. I was so mentally torn between right and wrong, the right thing to do would be to allow the police to arrest the guys who stabbed Darnel's friend. The wrong thing to do was justify that Darnel was within his rights to hurt the boys who had hurt his friend.

I'm not gonna lie, that night, evil won. I was staying with Darnel. I loved him.

Chapter Seven

CHRISTMAS DAY

Big Christmas day and I still hadn't spoken to Darnel for nearly 48 hours. He had texted me letting me know he was ok, but he hadn't answered any of my six missed calls. I was starting to feel a little like dumb Hazel again by running him down. I knew he was going through some serious shit, but still, how could I help him if he wasn't fully letting me in? Plus, I was sort of starting to question our relationship myself after all these recent events and thoughts, I mean, I did love him, but I was sort of starting to question how much I loved myself.

Today, all my family on my mum's side was coming over for a huge Christmas feast, but I wasn't really in the mood to celebrate. I felt sick, moody and mentally drained. Dragging myself out of bed, I heard my five-year-old little sister, Tammy, excitedly opening her presents. Joining my mum and sister in the living room, I was just in time to see the joy on her little face as she unwrapped the singing doll I had bought for her with some of the money Darnel had given me.

Tammy was my pride and joy who gave the best hugs in the world, the innocence in her was mind-blowing. Looking into her sweet little face, I smiled gently. "Thank you so much," Tammy went on to say that Jessica in her class has the same doll. "Really?" I replied, smiling understandingly. "So, who has the best big sister in the whole wide world?" "I do, I do," Tammy answered, jumping up and down with the widest grin. "Do you like the rest of your presents?" I continued.

"Yes, I love them all, mummy got me walkie talkies, look, can you play them with me?" She asked excitedly. "Sure," I replied, let me get dressed and we'll play them together later.

Once I was washed and dressed, I called Becks, Blessing and Nazarene to wish them all a Merry Christmas, then, as promised, went to play walkie talkies with Tammy. My headache was gone, and the sick feeling was subsiding. While helping my mum prepare the dinner for the family, I started to feel a bit better. I still hadn't heard from Darnel, but I had spoken to my good friends and no one had mentioned any madness on the road.

My favourite Uncle Terry, the comedian, was the first to arrive, shortly followed by my miserable Aunt Margret. Soon, the house was filled with all my family. The music was playing loud, the food as per usual was fantastic, we had turkey, lamb, chicken and duck, plus all the trimmings, stuffing, carrots, brussels sprouts, potatoes, pigs in blankets and Guinness punch. By the time we had all finished our dinners, our stomachs were stuffed.

All the grown-ups were merrily drinking away, the kids were playing nicely, it was such a good evening with a loving atmosphere, I almost forgot about all my recent anxieties and heartbreak. While in the middle of talking to Uncle Terry, Darnel called me.

Making my excuses quickly, I ran into the bathroom to answer the call. When I heard Darnel's voice, I remember thinking I'm not even sure if I should be talking to you, it was eleven o'clock and Christmas Day was nearly over, and he had only decided to call me back now. "Darnel, where have you been? How's Plastic, is he ok? Why haven't you answered any of my calls?" I blurted out, by now, the missed calls had increased to 10. "Come downstairs, babes, I'm outside."

Hanging up the phone, my ears were streaming, what was wrong with this dude? Why did he have to be so arrogant? Sometimes I just didn't get him, like why did he think he didn't need to answer any of my questions? Who did he think he was? I thought, quietly slipping out of my house. Making my way to the car, I had it all planned in my head, this was it, the new year was starting soon and this shit couldn't carry on, I wanted us to separate before then. He was getting deeper and deeper into more problems on the road and today, being around all my family had reminded me that I had come from a decent bunch and this chaotic life was not for me.

Taking a deep breath, I told myself, 'Vanessa, it is now or never,' I needed to do this before my heart had a chance to talk my head out of it. Plus, I needed to let him know I wanted him to take the gun and money out of my house. Pulling the door handle of the passenger's side, I spotted Joseph sitting in the back seat. For God's sake, did he seriously come to my house with his friend on Christmas Day? "Hi," I said, even more annoyed, trying not to show the real frustration I truly felt. "Yo, babes," Darnel said, "Merry Christmas," "thanks, same to you," I replied without turning my head to look at him.

"How's your day been?" he continued like he didn't realize or care that I was fuming, "yeah, it's been nice, my family has been here all day, how's your day been?" "Yeah, you know me, my day's been cool." By now, I knew in my heart I was making the right choice, the bastard hadn't called me for almost two days knowing I would be worrying like hell and then had the cheek to turn up on Christmas Day at 11 pm with his friend.

Turning to face him to let him know we were finished, I felt nervous, I didn't want to do this in front of his friend, but he had left me no choice by bringing him along. Looking down at his littered car floor, trying my best to think of the right thing to say, I looked back up barely catching my breath. In his hand was a small black jewellery box. "Babes, this is for you," my frustration melted instantly, I came over all flustered, can you believe he had gone out and bought me a beautiful white gold diamond ring?

OMG! I couldn't take the smile off my face, was he asking me to marry him? Was this a token of his love or a gesture to keep me cool? I wasn't sure or even bothered, but I knew then and there I wasn't going anywhere. "Thank you," I said, still grinning and overwhelmed by the ring.

Darnel was a man who didn't show many emotions, I had known that from the very moment I had met him, he was a "G", a mandem, but in my eyes, this was his way of letting me know he checked for me.

"I'm so sorry, I didn't buy you anything," I said completely embarrassed. "Don't worry, Vanessa, I didn't want you to buy me anything, it's cool." Chilling with him and Joseph for the next few minutes, I couldn't wait to get back inside to call Becks or Blessing to tell them about my diamond ring. Turning to Darnel and Joseph, I explained I needed to get back home to my family as they were probably leaving soon. Truth is, I was so frigging happy, I wanted to shout it out to the world. I was no longer upset he had brought his friend along; the more the merrier I say.

As I was shutting the car door, Darnel leaned over towards the passenger's side and told me to call him later when all my family had left because he needed to talk to me about something. My heart must have skipped about 99 beats. I couldn't believe my luck. He had given me my ring in front of his friend but wanted to ask me to marry him in private. "Ok, I'll call you later," I replied, trying my best to keep my composure. I swear I floated off on cloud nine back upstairs into my house.

"Where were you?" Aunty moody Margret called out when she saw me coming back in. "oh, umm, I went downstairs to meet..." I paused for a second, still smiling, not knowing how to respond, not sure if I should say boyfriend or fiancé. "oh, I went downstairs to meet my friend Becks to give her a Christmas present," I lied. "Hmmm really? Because I think your mum was calling you; we're all going soon," she said, trying to believe me. "oh, ok," I smirked, wanting them to hurry up and go home so I could call Darnel.

It was about 1 am before my last family member left my house. I felt so tired, but the adrenaline of the suspected proposal kept me wide awake. I had called Becks, Blessing and Nazarene and they all agreed they thought this might be my night. Becks, to be fair, was a little wary for me, she had been though from day one, it's not that she had anything personal against Darnel, but I guess sometimes she worried about me getting too caught up.

Calling Darnel, the butterflies in my stomach started to body pop, my throat was dry, and my knees felt weak, this was gonna be the perfect Christmas, the perfect end to a rocky few months. Becks needn't worry about me, I was finally gonna get what I deserved. "Hi, Darnel," I said once he had answered the phone, my heart raced, waiting to hear his undying love and then the words, 'will you marry me?' "Yo, Vanessa, you alright yeah?" "Yeah, thanks," I replied, grinning widely, "did you like your ring?" OMG, this was it, he was gonna do it now. "Yeah, thank you, I love the ring, sorry once again I didn't get you anything." "Don't worry, I told you it's cool."

"I've been meaning to talk to you about something from a couple of days ago, but because of all the madness happening on road, I forgot," I was grinning so hard, I thought my face would permanently stay this way. Ahh man, the way I was picturing our big day full of love with all our family and friends congratulating us, it's nuts. "Ok, go on," I prompted so very excited. "Vanessa, when was your last period?" Wait, what was he on about? When I tell you the total confusion, I felt is an understatement. What did my last period have to do with a marriage proposal? "Umm, I'm not sure," I responded, caught completely by surprise, "why do you ask?" "I've been spitting a lot and think you or someone else may be pregnant for me."

Me or someone else? So how many girls was he sleeping with? I stayed silent, I felt like I'd been kicked in the stomach, my head began to spin. Right now, I should have been saying yes and setting our wedding date, but instead, I had just been told that I or someone else may be pregnant for him. What would I say to Becks, Blessing and Nazarene tomorrow when they asked me excitedly how it all went? How could I tell them that there had been no proposal but pure disrespect?

Why had he done this to me? NO, actually, why did I do this to myself? This wasn't the first time he had made me feel like shit, but time and time again, I had allowed myself to be drawn back in. I was completely lost for words. How do you respond to such a mad statement such as 'you or someone else might be pregnant for me'?

Taking a deep breath, I didn't have the energy to let him know he had deeply hurt me. He had given me a diamond ring and, of course, I stupidly thought he was gonna ask me to marry him; what girl wouldn't? You see, that was the trouble with girls like me, completely missing the true meaning behind these types of guys. Not wanting to make a big deal out of what he had said tonight, I just said, "goodnight, I'll speak to you tomorrow."

Chapter Eight

ENOUGH IS ENOUGH

Over the remainder of the festive holidays, I couldn't shake off the thought that someone else or myself may be pregnant. The words kept playing over and over again in my mind like a shitty broken record. The thought of having a baby at my age was crazy. I mean, I did feel sick some of the time, but I put that down to stress. I'd never actually vomited, so surely if I had been pregnant, I would have noticed, or there would've been some sort of tell-tell signs.

After that hurtful stunt on what should've been my magical proposal night, I tried my best to distance myself from Darnel. When he would call me, I started out trying to be strong and let the phone ring out, telling myself I was better off without him. In truth, that would only last for 1 or 2 missed calls. Although he had disrespected me, like an idiot, again and again I would make excuses as to why he had done it and hoped that he would change.

The roads around this time became manic. Ever since the incident with Plastic and Slimzy, Darnel had become colder than ever. Although Plastic was now thankfully on the mend, Darnel refused to let things go. I was getting phone calls left, right and centre from different friends, one time, a friend called Marsha had gone out to a house party where she saw Darnel and some of his entourage. I'm not even totally sure what went on but rumour had it that an argument had broken out with another rival gang, shots were fired back and forth, leaving a member of the rival gang on life support and then brain dead.

Not only was his crew in beef with the boys who stabbed Plastic, but they seemed to be taking over the streets by storm. Anybody and everybody who made money selling drugs or fraud would be robbed or taxed. I kept a low profile around this time, not wanting to get caught by one of Darnel's enemies, these situations just kept escalating. One part of me felt very protected but the other half felt so vulnerable.

Once I returned to school, my period still hadn't come. From time to time when I spoke to Darnel, he would ask me and I would let him know it still hadn't come as yet, believing it would. When another week or so passed with no period still in sight, I confided in Becks and Nazarene who said they would come to the clinic with me. The next day, we bunked our last lessons and went to a clinic just off West Green Road in Tottenham.

I remember on our arrival the three of us went in like most normal teenagers just joking around. The nurse I saw gave me a white plastic cup to pee in, instead of giving the cup straight back to the nurse, I found myself back in the waiting room, pretending to throw the wee on Becks. Some of the wee flew out of the cup and landed on the floor, so we all burst out laughing. When I eventually went in to see the nurse, I wasn't nervous at all, I truly believed Darnel must have been mistaken, how could he even know what was going on in my body just because he'd been spitting? He had to be mistaken.

As I sat down, I watched as the nurse put on a pair of white gloves then took something that looked like a syringe and dipped it in my wee, she then put a few drops onto the pregnancy test. While we waited, she asked me a few questions like what my age was, when my last period was, which I couldn't remember, and within a few seconds went on to say, "yes, the test is positive." I was eight weeks pregnant. Eight weeks! I couldn't believe what I was hearing; was she sure?

I sat there like a completely different person to who had first walked through those clinic doors. My hands now covering my whole face. Darnel had been right, I was indeed pregnant, how did I get myself in this situation? Well, I knew how, but still, I wasn't ready for a baby. I could see the nurse looking at me with zero empathy, her expression said it all, if you were woman enough to have sex, then you should be woman enough to deal with the consequences.

Walking back into the waiting area to Becks and Nazarene, I never said a word. I didn't have to really; they could see the total shock plastered all over my face. My mind kept telling me this couldn't be real; how would I cope? I was far too young to have a child. I was still a child myself. My friends tried to reassure me that everything would be ok and that they would be there for me no matter what. Leaving the clinic, I was in a daze, the only real person I needed to be there for me was the person who had got me in this situation.

Straight after school the following day, I called Darnel to let him know I wanted to see him. Arriving at his house, he was in a good mood. Great, I thought, I may as well get this over with, "Um, Darnel, you know you was asking me the other day about my period? Well, I went and took a test and it came out positive."

Darnel never said a word, just stared blankly at me. "Darnel, say something," I said, rolling my eyes but searching his face at the same time. Darnel's face broke out into the happiest grin I had ever seen from him. My eyes shot open, "Oh, you're happy?" I said, shocked. "Course I am, babes, come here, man," reaching out to hug me. I couldn't believe it, I half expected him to ask me to have an abortion, but he was genuinely happy.

We hugged for about the next 20 minutes, it felt so special, he kept telling me how happy he was, asking me questions like how far gone I was, if I was happy and when was I gonna tell my mum because he was planning on telling his mum soon. This guy who I had fallen in love with was heavy, this guy who I loved was cold, but he was the one I was giving a baby to and definitely now my soul.

After about two hours of me being with Darnel, he received a phone call which put him in a real foul mood, I didn't even hear all the conversation as he was walking in and out of the front room. I heard him say something like, "what do you mean he's lost the food?" Darnel was shouting at the top of his voice, saying, "nah, he's chatting shit," he walked back out, so I lost the rest of the conversation. Coming back into the front room, I dare not ask him what was wrong, he just sat down for about five minutes staring, deep in thought, and then walked back out. I wanted to ask him what was wrong. I hated seeing him so wound up, it made me feel uneasy and awkward.

Pretending to be engrossed in EastEnders, I watched out of the corner of my eye as Darnel called somebody else. "Yo, guess what that f**king prick Damien did? He lost twelve grand worth of food." For a moment, he was quiet, listening to the response the person was giving, just nodding and grunting. Without warning, he jumped up, startling me, and started shouting down the phone, "that's what I'm talking about, he's chatting shit, do them pricks think I'm one of them?" Rage in his face, he walked straight back out the front room.

Turning my attention back to EastEnders, I could see on the TV screen Sharon being exposed in the pub for sleeping with her boyfriend, Grant's brother, Phil. Just then, Darnel walked back into the front room, picked up his other phone on the settee and walked back out again. From where I was sat, I could hear Darnel now in the hallway rummaging around, looking for something and then silence.

It was another fifteen minutes before he reappeared, interrupting my daydreams about the whole evening. "Put your shoes on, we're going down the road," he said abruptly. "Where we going?" I began to question. "Please just hurry up and put on your shoes," Darnel demanded. I put on my shoes and hurried after him, now stood by the front door with a small plastic bag wrapped around his wrist.

Walking towards the parked black Golf GTI, no words were exchanged. Driving along Tottenham

High Road, we sat in total silence for I still dared not ask him what was wrong. I could only imagine he had brought me out to get some food to calm down or check one of his friends to rant and rave about Damien losing the drugs... how wrong I was!

Pulling up on a dirt road in Enfield, I looked on closely as Darnel pulled the small plastic black bag he had hid under his seat when we first got in the car and take out a black woolly hat and leather gloves. I was completely nervous when I saw a small silver gun come out also. Once he had everything ready, he turned to me and said, "come, come, come." "Where to?" I asked, not able to hide the enormity of fear. "I said come." Man, I knew he was angry but what did that have to do with me? I hadn't lost his food, "come on," he repeated. Against my will, I stepped out of the car feeling like I wanted to faint.

Walking along, my legs wobbled beneath me. When we were a few doors down from where he'd parked, Darnel ordered me to knock the red door we were stood in front of. "Huh? No, I'm not knocking any door, please let's just go back to the car," I began to plead. "Are you deaf? I said to knock the red door." I'm certain in that moment I saw the devil himself. I wanted to tell him to f**k off, why didn't he knock the red door if he wanted the bloody door knocked so badly? Looking into his hands, I could see he had his gun ready.

This situation was showing his true colours by the second. We were outside one of his enemies' houses and he wanted me to knock the f**king red door. So, when his enemy opened the door, he would open fire. "No, please, I don't want to knock the door," I began to beg. By the demented look I received, I knew I had no choice. Slowly, I started to walk towards the door I was forced to knock. Glancing back, Darnel was now hidden behind a hedge.

Ok, so, scenario 1, this is how it would be; I ring the bell, some unknown man opens the door; Darnel tries to shoot at him but shoots me in the back and I wind up dead.

Scenario 2, I ring the doorbell, some unknown man opens the door, he has a gun in his hand and the pair have a shootout.

F**k this for a laugh, neither of the two scenarios was good for me, no matter which way I looked at it, I would wind up dead tonight if I knocked on the door.

Continuing to walk ever so slowly towards the red door, my blood was red hot. Who gave this mother f**ker the right to choose my fate? He was supposed to love and protect me, what was that all about 3 hours ago when he told me he was happy I was pregnant? How could he be happy but put us both at risk? Reaching the front door, I decided I wasn't gonna do what he wanted me to do, there was no way on God's earth I would be the one to call someone to their death.

Nah, the more these ridiculous thoughts were flying through my mind, the more I knew I had to do whatever it took to protect myself, shielding the door with my entire body I pretended to ring the doorbell, looking slightly around at Darnel, praying he was convinced I had done it. Standing there for a couple of seconds, my heart was thumping. Darnel called out in a low voice, telling me to ring the doorbell again.

Once again, I did what I had to do, pretended to ring the bell hoping no one would catch me, only just then, the hallway light went on. How the f**k did they know I was there? I hadn't really rung the bell. My mind was screaming at me to run and never look back, but my legs couldn't move. I stood still, rooted to the spot, the diarrhoea threatening to fall out my bum cheeks. I could hear slow footsteps approaching the door, how I never fainted is still a mystery to me.

As the door opened, I held my breath, only to find a Turkish old man with a bin bag in his hands coming from flat A, when the man saw me stood on his doorstep, we both jumped, the relief that washed over me only God knows. I apologised to the elderly man and explained I had mistaken his house for one of my friend's houses. The man seemed to accept my explanation and with that, I turned around and left.

When I got back in the car, I couldn't control my anger, I completely exploded. I started lashing out, trying to kick and punch Darnel as hard as I could. I was so mad, I screamed. Who gave him the right to put me in such a vulnerable situation? I kept repeating myself over and over again, telling him we were over, and I couldn't be with someone who would put me at such a high risk.

He had never seen me so angry and, to be fair, I don't think I had ever been so angry with him, but I was sure our relationship was definitely over. Darnel was full of remorse, saying he was sorry and he didn't know what had come over him, a part of me felt a tiny bit sorry for him, but still, he had truly not given a shit about us, so there was no going back.

When we got outside my house, I jumped out of the car without saying bye. Darnel wound down his window and tried to call me back, but I held my head straight and didn't look back. This time he had done it, he had gone too far, he had hurt me deeply and I just needed time and space.

Chapter Nine

FACING REALITY

"Are you sure this is what you want? You're only sixteen, how you gonna manage? How are you gonna support a baby? Have you thought this all through cause from where I'm sitting, you don't have a clue about what you gonna do, do you? Vanessa, Vanessa, I'm talking to you, what are you gonna say to your teachers for Pete's sake? How you gonna buy baby stuff when you don't have a job?" Sitting on the big black dressing table chair, I could hear my mum's voice trailing off in the background whilst I was inwardly sighing.

"Mum, I understand what you are trying to say..." Before I could even finish my sentence, my mum butted in, "No you don't, you're not fully grasping the concept of what I'm trying to explain to you, you don't understand," "Mum, look," "No,

Vanessa, you look, let me put this to you bluntly so you understand exactly what I'm telling you, lots of young guys don't stick around for long, they ain't in this for the long run."

"Do you really think he will be there for you when your baby wakes up at night or needs changing? Do you truly believe you can rely on him? Please, Vanessa, I just need you to understand that this journey you're about to embark on will be the hardest journey of your life. Do you know how hard it was for me practically raising you and now your little sister by myself? Let me tell you, it's been bloody hard, so I know what I'm talking about! I don't want you or Tammy to go through any of the struggles I've been through."

"You know it's not too late for you to have an abortion if you want to, you're only two and a half months, so there's still time." Here we go again; I was waiting for my mum to say that. In the past two weeks, she had found out I was pregnant. She had subtly tried to persuade me to have an abortion. Taking a deep breath, I lifted my head which hung in shame from the dark grey carpet I had been looking at for the past half an hour.

Looking directly into my mum's broken eyes with rising panic beating away at my chest, I replied, "mum, I want this baby and there's no way I'm having an abortion. Seriously, please don't be angry with me, I didn't want or expect this to happen but now it has, I have to take responsibility for my actions." "Ok, Vanessa, if your mind is made up, what can I say? Just be prepared for all the things I warned you about. I don't want you to think I was pressuring you into having an abortion, but I needed you to know the option was there if you wanted it," she replied softly.

"I'm not gonna lie, I'm heartbroken and devastated, but no matter what, you're my daughter, so I'll stand by you, come here," her eyes looked longingly at me as she held her arms open. I so wanted to bury myself in her arms. OMG, my subconscious was screaming out at me, why in the hell did you get yourself into this predicament? Look long and hard at your mum, she's been so good to you, why you gonna go and break her heart? Go away and leave me alone, subconscious, I'm not doing this to hurt anybody, least of all my mum.

Leaving my mum's room, I caught a glimpse of her reflection in the wardrobe mirror, by now, her head was bent down and I could see a steady stream of tears splashing onto her white bedspread. Nervously clutching my small but growing belly, I truly felt terrible. If only I could have been honest with my mum and told her deep down I knew she was probably right, or the fact I knew he was actively sleeping with other people and we weren't even talking, but no, I couldn't, I had just betrayed the one person in the world who loved me so dearly.

Walking into my bedroom, I lay down on my single bed and began to silently cry. I sat there for a couple of hours just thinking back over the last few months, asking myself how I got myself into this mess. How was it that in the next six or so months, I was to become a mother? A part of me wanted to run into my mum's room and tell her she was right and I was making the biggest mistake of my life, but the other part of me kept thinking about the unborn child I so already loved.

Going into the kitchen a couple of hours later once I had pulled myself together, to the aroma of rice and peas and chicken. My belly rumbled letting me know how hungry I was. I almost forgot the conversation I'd had with my mum earlier. She looked so worn out, she looked like she hadn't stopped crying for the last couple of hours I'd spent in my room. "Mum, is the dinner ready cause I'm starving?" salivating as the smell overtook me. "Yeah, it is," experience told me my mum was still very upset, the atmosphere felt very odd.

Sighing heavily, I dished out a plate of food whilst trying to suppress the deep feelings of guilt which plagued me. "Mum, do you mind if I go and stay at Theresa's house tonight?" Theresa was one of my mum's best friends and one of the easiest adults to talk to. My mum replied without even looking at me in a sarcastic tone, "I think that's for the best as I need some space."

Packing the few things I needed to go to Theresa's house, I travelled light. I had stayed at Theresa's house often before I met Darnel, so there wasn't much I needed that wasn't already there. Tomorrow was a new day, I kept telling myself, just let the dust settle a bit with mumsy and everything will be alright.

Reaching Theresa's house, I spent some time explaining I was pregnant and how much hurt I'd caused my mum. Talking with Theresa made me feel like a weight had been lifted off my shoulders. This is what I loved about her, she was hassle-free, she just let me talk freely, no pressure or hassle, just an open ear.

Relaxing to a bowl of Rice Krispies with Jerry Springer blasting from the TV, I started to feel a little better. Today had been a hard day, but now everything was out in the open with my mum, things could start to get better. Switching over the TV to see what else was on, my mobile started to ring, on the screen flashed mum. My gosh, I had only been gone for a couple of hours, did she really wanna go over the fact I was too young to have a baby again?

"Hi, mum," I began, "you at Theresa's?" my mum interrupted, sounding panicked. "Yeah, why what's wrong?" "Vanessa, I'm coming to get you now!" "Why?" I asked again, starting to feel panicked myself. "Because something happened to Darnel and he's here. Meet me at the end of Theresa's flats, I'm leaving now." "What happened?" "Vanessa, I'm not sure, just meet me now." Jumping to my feet, my mind began to do summersaults. What the hell could have happened to him and why was he at my mum's house? We hadn't spoken in two weeks since the day he asked me to knock on that f**king red door. Pushing my thoughts to the back of my mind, for now, I needed to make sure he was ok and find out what had gone on. Shouting upstairs to Theresa, I let her know I was leaving to go back home; I didn't even wait for a response, I was straight out the door.

Within minutes, my mum came screeching around the corner, something had to be serious, my mum never drove this fast. Jumping in the car, my questions came thick and fast; "what happened? Is he ok? How did he end up at our house?" "I'm not sure, all I know is sometime after you left, the doorbell kept ringing and ringing, I opened the window to see who was ringing the bell like that and it was Darnel just standing there. I shouted out the window that you weren't here, but he shouted back asking if I could still open the door."

"When I let him in, I could see some blood on his shirt, he looked scared and that's when he asked if I could get you." Reaching home with uncertainty swimming through my whole body, I couldn't run up the stairs fast enough. Sitting in front of me was a sight for sore eyes, for the first time, I saw real fear. Darnel was sitting in silence, staring into space with a concerned expression from deep within his soul.

Looking directly, I could see an open hole in his arm levelled to his heart, I had never seen a bullet wound before, but I knew straight away that this was almost definitely caused by a bullet. My heart sank, I couldn't believe how close he had come to death, a few inches to the right and he would have been a goner. Dropping to my knees, sitting directly in front of him, I didn't know what to do. "What happened, Darnel?" I asked softly, "Nothing just a little madness and some prick shot me in my arm."

I caught sight of my mum as the word 'shot' left Darnel's mouth. My mum started choking on her drink, she looked like she had seen the walking dead. If looks could kill, I would've been dead. I knew I had some explaining to do. But for now, I needed to focus all my attention on Darnel.

"We need to get you to the hospital, you're hurt, we need to get you stitched up," I continued. "No, it's cool, my aunt is a nurse so I'll go and see her tomorrow," he replied faintly. "Are you sure cos I think you need to get your arm checked out tonight," "No, I said I'm fine. Do you think your mum will mind if I chill here for a couple of hours?" "No, my mum will be fine," I lied, knowing after my mum heard the word shot and madness, she probably wanted him out of the house now!

Still not knowing what to do, I went and fetched a towel to wrap around his swollen arm as there was still a little bit of blood oozing. "Do you want a drink or anything to eat?" I asked. Although I was still very concerned about how close he had come to death, I was trying to keep things as normal as possible. "Yeah, get me a Ribena please if you have it." "Let me check," I smiled, walking into the kitchen, my mum was still in there, her eyes still resembling those of someone who had seen something frightening.

"Vanessa, did I hear Darnel say he got shot? What the hell's going on? Why would someone shoot him?" she asked, completely naïve to Darnel's lifestyle. I could see confusion and many more questions plastered all over her face. "Mum, don't worry, it was just a silly argument with one of Darnel's friends but unfortunately he got hurt."

I walked back to Darnel with a pint glass of Ribena held in my hand. I know this may sound silly and it probably wasn't the right time, but somehow, I felt special. He had come to me in his hour of need, even though we weren't talking. Walking over to the video player, I inserted the film, Belly, and sat down next to my Mr Handsome. From now on, everything was gonna be alright; it had to be.

Chapter Ten

THE RAID

Over the next couple of weeks, life with Darnel was bliss for a while. My mum wasn't very keen on me staying out at his house some nights, but the damage was already done, I was 3 months and 1 week pregnant, plus I still knew she would want some sort of explanation about Darnel being shot. I tried my best to nurse him back to health, which didn't take very long as he was a soldier, a warrior, he didn't allow anything to hold him down.

There were days where we would spend the whole day together like an old married couple, totally in love or just fooling around. Occasionally, I swear to you he was like the coolest guy on earth, he could be so loving, a side to him most rarely saw, but

I did, I saw it at times. Deep down, at heart, I knew he was a good guy. Over those couple of weeks, he constantly reminded me of how much he loved me, and our unborn child would want for nothing.

Darnel wasn't a mean man, but I also wasn't a greedy girl, I didn't want or need lots of money from him, I just wanted us to be like any other normal couple. When I first met him, I knew he wasn't a dickhead but to be fair what girl wants a dickhead guy in their life? I honestly thought I could manage him somehow, tame him even, but for the most part, that definitely wasn't true, I just hoped and prayed that the bullet wound and our relationship would be enough to make him rethink about his life and what he really wanted.

There were also days when I would be chilling in the bedroom with about 10 man all sitting in his house discussing their enemies. I tried talking to him several times about changing his lifestyle, but he was just so stuck in his ways. There was this one day I was too tired to go school, so I decided to go over to Darnel's house at about midday for a little nap. I walked into the kitchen and saw eight man all tightly squeezed, sitting together around the kitchen table with each of them having their gun placed just in front of them, and Darnel standing, leading the pack. I became nervous and after 15 minutes, I made my excuses and left.

I was becoming a little fed up with wanting him to change, I mean, I didn't want him to be a nerd or anything like that, but at the same time, I couldn't emphasise the fact enough that we had a child on the way, I so wanted a normal life where one day I would come home from work and shout out, "honey, I'm home," but the more I stayed around Darnel, the more danger I was putting us in. Sometimes my mind drifted to all sorts of places like one of his enemies trying to kill me or my baby, or even one day I would get a flat of my own whilst he continued to leave his shit at my house and then the house would get raided and the child would end up in care.

The more I thought about these horrible and wicked thoughts, the more I kept telling myself I needed to get away from this shitty lifestyle, but then it only took one word, or a single romantic touch and I was hooked all over again.

I didn't have to wait long for the horrible thoughts to become reality. One of the nights while

I was staying over at Darnel's house, I wasn't really feeling well so I decided to go to bed a little early, I woke up about half twelve dying to go to the toilet. While walking on the landing towards the toilet, I could hear soft music playing while Darnel was on the phone talking, almost in a whisper, this made my ears prick up, when I heard the words, "babes, don't be like that, you know I've got love for you," with a little smirk in his voice, I almost fell over. My heart started hammering dramatically fast.

I really wanted to listen to the rest of the conversation, but something took over my mouth, it really did, it was like I was having an out-of-body experience. I couldn't believe he had me here pregnant in his house while he had the nerve to be speaking to another bitch on the phone while I slept. How dare he do that to me. I started shouting at the top of my voice, you name it, I called him it, he turned around and hung up the phone so fast, I'm not even sure if the girl he was speaking to even realised what was going on.

I couldn't stop the tears escaping from my eyes, how could he be doing this to me? I thought he loved me, well, I really loved him, I had sacrificed so much for him, I still even had some of his shit in my house, risking myself and my family for this prick, only for him to be chatting shit to another girl while I slept. I really wondered if he'd done this to me any other time, I'd fallen asleep before him.

I stormed back in the bedroom and started to pick up all the belongings I had brought with me over the last couple of weeks. I was so devastated but this was long, I was done with him, the tears were still running down my cheeks, the bogeys starting to leak on my face, I didn't even care. My whole world had just crumbled right in front of my eyes.

The apologies were coming thick and fast, "Vanessa, babes, don't be like that, I'm sorry, man, come give me a hug," I don't know why but after a couple of hours, I stupidly calmed down and we started to talk, we talked until about half 3 in the morning, I can't believe I allowed myself to forgive him so easily but he promised me it would never happen again. He was the one causing me the pain, but he was also the one I loved and felt I needed to be comforted by.

I must have drifted off through exhaustion, but the next thing I knew, I was awoken about half

6 in the morning to the loud crashing noise of the front door being smashed in. I panicked, I could hear the footsteps running up the stairs towards the direction of the bedroom where me and Darnel slept. Ohhh my days, my mind was screaming out at me, why didn't you go home when you caught the bastard speaking to another girl?

My legs wobbled once again, threatening to give away beneath me. As the door flew open, I heard a number of officers shouting out, "Police, stay where you are, get down, get down," I looked at Darnel, whose face was screwed up like he was pissed that they had interrupted his sleep. I stood still, I couldn't move, an officer grabbed my arms like he wanted to wrestle or handcuff me.

Then and there, right where I stood, I threw up, I wasn't sure if Darnel had been under surveillance or even me for a matter of fact, but my nerves of knowing what was in my house kept me bent over, spilling my guts, for what felt like a few minutes. All I knew was I needed to do whatever it took to keep some distance between my mum's house and these police. Could you imagine the police searching my room and finding the stuff neatly hidden behind my wardrobe? My poor mum would defo have a heart attack, being arrested for firearms and drugs, something she knew nothing about. I swear these thoughts must've made me pass out for a bit because when I came around, a female officer was stood over me, calling my name.

I came round to Darnel still dressed only in his boxing shorts, handcuffed and being led out the bedroom whilst cursing the officers, "Get the f**k off me, man, I told you already I don't have anything, leave her alone she's f**king pregnant." The lady officer still stood in front of me offered me a glass of water which I refused; my head was still trying to grasp what was really going on here.

"So, Vanessa's your name," the officer continued. Looking around, there were different officers coming and going, some old, some young, my mind was struggling to take this all in, "yeah," I replied facing away from her, I was nervous as hell, I still wasn't sure what I needed to say here, did she know my name because she heard Darnel calling me or did she know my name already cos I was implicated to him? The least I said, the better I guessed. "So, we're here on suspicion of drugs," "Suspicion of drugs?" I repeated, looking completely astonished. All the thoughts I had 2 seconds ago about not saying anything vanishing, "are you sure you've come to the right address?" I asked, swallowing hard, "yep, we have," the female officer continued.

What choice did I have? I could've stayed quiet, but to be quite frank, I knew I needed to do an Oscar-winning performance, "sorry, officer, please come again," I continued very convincingly, "did you really just say drugs?" The lady officer looked at me from head to toe, trying to suss out my facial expression as if she was unsure as to whether I was an innocent party in all these affairs or a liar. "Yes," she repeated, "I said we're here to find drugs, so I heard Darnel say you're pregnant, is that true?" "Yes, it is," "and how many months are you, my lovely?" I didn't know if I should tell the truth or say I lie, I looked straight at the two male officers who were in the room stood by the doorway also trying to read me, "umm, nearly three months." Well, it was only a small little white lie, I was just over three months.

"So, where do you live, Vanessa?" the women officer asked with a friendly but concerned expression, my mind quickly flashed to the movies I had previously watched in the past with this good cop, bad cop shit, there was no way I was gonna allow one of these officers to trick me into believing they cared about me. "Umm, I live with my mum but ever since she found out I was pregnant, she's kicked me out, so that's why I'm here."

"So, how old are you?" "I'm 16," "You're still a baby," she frowned, looking a bit sorry for me. "Let me give you some friendly advice, I don't know if you know much about the guy that you're with, but he's a criminal, don't throw away your whole life on a guy like this, I can tell you're a smart girl and you can do so much better." Seriously, did this woman just disrespect the father of my child in front of me? I was so surprised, I almost wanted to laugh but continued to listen and kept my composure.

The lecture lasted the whole time until the other officers finished the rest of the search, I must have done a proper Oscar performance I thought because while this officer lady tried to persuade me to not throw away my life on Darnel, she mentioned she would get a squad car to drop me home. I'd cried a bit and then told her I no longer wanted to be with him but needed to talk to him about things first, so I was fine and would make my own way home a little later. This didn't stop her taking down my address and contact details for if she needed it in the future.

Once the officers had finished their search and found absolutely nothing, they released Darnel from the handcuffs that were still tight around his wrists and told us to contact the council to get the door fixed, leaving the search warrant on the kitchen table as they left. Darnel's face was like thunder. He was mad as hell, but at the same time, happy they'd gone empty-handed. I swear he must have rung everybody in his phone book telling them what had just happened. I sat in silence for a while just letting all these thoughts and emotions swim around my head whilst I cleaned up the vomit and had a shower. What would have seriously happened if there had been anything here?

He was delighted but I was scared, scared these police officers could still go to my mum's and turn the place over. That lady officer had all my details and she seemed like she meant business, at one point, I swear she even mentioned this wasn't over. "Darnel, Darnel, are you ready?" I asked frantically an hour after the boys in blue had left, my head feeling like it was about to explode. "Ready?" he asked confused, "Ready to go where? I'm going back to bed I'm tired and you need to come back to bed as well." "Bed?" I jumped up shouting, alarming him, was this dude joking or what? "Darnel, we need to go to my mum's asap and move the stuff, we can't leave it there, seriously, we can't, imagine they search my mum's house right now. Please, we need to move the stuff to somewhere else."

My Mr handsome stared at me momentarily like I was talking another language, or maybe he was just figuring out the best way to convince me otherwise. "Vanessa, calm down, you know I love you, right?" I stayed quiet, hanging on to his every word, "Ness, you know I love you and would never let anything happen to you, right? The police won't go to your house, you're not known to the police, you've never been arrested and you don't have any criminal records, so I promise you you're cool." He must've seen the uncertainty still within my eyes, "Babes, honestly that's why I love you so much, thank you for all you do for me, don't think I don't appreciate it cos I do and that's why, one day, I'm gonna make you my wife. Seriously, Ness, come back to bed, it's all gonna be ok, I promise you."

Chapter Eleven

FATE

The raid last week must've increased my paranoia because I became jumpy as hell. Every time I left the house to go to school or even the shops, I felt as though I was being followed. Darnel did exactly what it took, or should I say, probably what I wanted to hear, to reassure me that everything was fine and I had nothing to worry about, he even went as far as to promise he would move his shit out of my house in a couple of weeks for good.

With this in mind, I decided not to dwell on everything and just get on with my everyday life. Recently, I had spent so much time with my Mr Handsome, I so needed to be around some of my friends and try and focus on my GCSEs that were taking place in only a few months. I had a purpose, my baby, to make sure I came out with the best grades I could.

That weekend, I stayed the night at Becks' house with Blessing which was just what the doctor ordered. I couldn't remember the last time I'd laughed that much and just felt like an ordinary teenager. A part of me for a short while even forgot I was pregnant, I so nearly lit up a cigarette, I even put it to my mouth, but then the mother's instincts inside of me kicked right back in.

That night, we talked until the small hours of the morning, we talked about everything except Darnel, they did try questioning me about how things were going and what had I been up to, but I just kept it brief by saying he was overjoyed about the baby and things were going smooth.

At one point, Blessing asked about Hazel, but I just shut it down by pretending I didn't hear. It's not that I was purposely trying to lie or hide things from my friends, but I just didn't know where to start or if they had heard anything on the road about him. Plus, I had come here to have some me-time. If I told them I had caught him talking to another girl which wasn't even Hazel and then about his house being raided but he still had drugs in my house, we definitely wouldn't have gone to sleep at all.

Getting home that Sunday after I left Becks' house, I felt my old self returning, yeah, I was gonna be a mum, but things just seemed clearer. I mean, I felt happier. I knew what I needed to do, which was to dedicate the next few months working hard towards getting good marks in my GCSEs and then focus on this baby; with or without Darnel. I had some good friends and family that loved me, so what more could I ask for? The icing on the cake would be if Darnel turned this lifestyle around, but either way, I knew what I needed to do.

For the next two weeks, I stuck to the plan except for the day I had to leave school early to go to a scan appointment which I went to with my mum. That scan appointment was magical, well, I mean, a real reality check. I saw my baby and heard its heartbeat for the first time, other than that, I was up and out, going to school every day early. Over this time, I hardly saw Darnel as I was trying to show him I was good with or without him, I did want us to be together, but I had to show him I was serious.

Friday evening, almost two weeks after the raid, I'd arranged to go over to Becks' house to do some studying with her and Blessing but then decided to go straight home as I was tired and felt confident to do the work alone. Earlier on, I'd got a devastating text from another friend that Pauline's mum only had 48 hours to live, so I felt really sad and not in a good mood at all.

Nearing the corner of my road, I noticed a few police cars parked near my house. Not paying much attention to it, I continued to walk on, just assuming the squad cars must have been for the hostel a few doors down. Over the last couple of years, the police had been called to that address several times.

As I got closer, I noticed a big blue van that read 'BBC NEWS' on it. I remember thinking whatever has happened at that flat must have been big news for the BBC to be present. I stopped dead in my tracks when I arrived at my gates to see the front door wide open and three police officers stood there chatting amongst themselves, not even noticing me. A part of me in my mind had already started running, the shock and terror that instantly crushed my stomach, I cannot tell you how I didn't lose my baby on the spot.

I seriously was about to turn around and start sprinting but where would I go? I didn't have any money or anywhere else permanent to stay. I would be evil to leave my mum in hot water, my body felt DEAD, I was empty inside, the words, "What's happening here?" just blurted out from my stupid mouth. The officer closest to me turned and looked and then said, "Sorry, who are you, do you live here?" I so wanted to say, 'nope, sorry, officer, continue your conversation,' but it was too late, I had opened up a can of worms I knew couldn't be closed and, besides, I had to face whatever these bastards were about to throw at me one way or the other.

"Yeah, I live here, what's going on?" I replied whilst trying to walk past the officer into my house. I was hoping just by some miracle I could be allowed in my room by myself and throw the stupid rucksack over to my neighbour's back yard. "Where's my mum?" I demanded, "Why are you here? Is everything ok?" I had to pretend if only for a little while I didn't know why they were there.

The young black officer who was dressed in plainclothes stopped me before I had a chance to put my foot on the steps. "Your mum and little sister are fine, they're in the kitchen. What's your name and how old are you?" My mind was stuck, the words just wouldn't come out, my mind was solely focused on Darnel and this horrible predicament he had put me in.

Darnel had promised me that everything would be ok, and I had trusted him. I didn't know how long these police officers had been searching my house. What I did know was that there was a rucksack full of his drugs, a handgun, bullets and about four grand in cash. Damn, I'd been caught, this game was up, I had been stupid. I told him from the time his house got raided I wanted him to move his shit and what did he do? Nothing but convince me that I was the one he loved and trusted. I was so angry at him but even more angry at myself. Pauline's mum, my second mum, only had a matter of hours to live and here I was about to be arrested.

When I reached the top of the stairs, who did I see with a smug cheeky grin staring at me? The lady officer from two weeks ago in Darnel's house. As I was being led into the front room, we passed the kitchen where I saw my mum and Tammy sitting patiently, waiting for the search to be over. I looked straight at my mum as if to say I'm so SORRY, but she just cut her eye and turned her head.

I must have sat down for literally 30 seconds when I heard an officer who was upstairs in one of the bedrooms at the top of the house call out, "Sarg, come up please, I think we found something," the lady officer glanced over at me and then made her way upstairs. My heart stopped beating, trust me it did, all the hopes and promises I'd made over the last couple of weeks disappeared. I almost shouted out, 'I'm sorry, this has nothing to do with my mum and little sis, it's all me.' The camera crew flew out the kitchen with a massive camera in hand, repositioning in the hallway for the police to come back downstairs. I closed my eyes and let out the biggest sigh I have ever done in my life, all my anxieties and fears choking me at once.

I heard the footsteps slowly moving down the stairs and, still, I kept my eyes tightly closed, I had allowed what happened to Pauline to finally happen to me, it was only when I heard that blasted woman's voice that I reopened my eyes. "Well, well, well, what do we have here?" the words, 'let me explain again' almost slipped from my tongue, I couldn't believe what I was looking at, my eyes nearly fell out of my head when I saw she was holding up a small bag of weed that looked like it didn't even cost a fiver. The officer searched my face for answers. I searched right back at hers, not understanding why that was all she had in her hand, both of us not quite sure where all the answers lay.

The camera crew looked so pissed off, it was unreal, like they wanted something to be found;

idiots. I couldn't understand what was going on, I had been home for at least ten minutes now, of which they had spent most of their time upstairs. How had they not found the bag? It's not like I had hidden it superbly well or hidden it under any floorboards, it was just behind my wardrobe with a jumper on top covering it.

As soon as I could see them getting ready to leave, I became a little cocky. I asked the woman officer what she was doing in my house and told her I wanted to take this further on police harassment. I explained to her in no uncertain terms that she was only here because of the colour of my skin. She tried to explain some rubbish or the other, letting me know she could arrest me on suspicion of finding a class B drug with intent to supply, what a joke, but I was having none of it, I just wanted them out of my house so I could sort shit out.

Once everyone had left, I apologised to my mum, letting her know I didn't understand why they had come to our address, it had to be some sort of a mistake, and then made my way straight upstairs to behind the wardrobe. To my astonishment, there was no black rucksack in sight, they had clearly gone through all my draws and belongings, but there was no rucksack.

Chapter Twelve

ULTIMATUM

I stared up at the ceiling completely puzzled, trying to comprehend the massive situation at hand, where was this frigging bag? This had to be a joke for which I was defo missing the punch line. My whole existence once again became drained, can you imagine there had to have been literally up to about fifteen officers and the BBC, but yet no one had found the bag. Racking my brains good and hard, I honestly couldn't remember the last time Darnel had asked me to give or bring him anything out of it. It must've only been around a week or two ago, but for the life of me, I just couldn't remember.

Maybe this was an absolute miracle of some sort, what else could be the explanation? It just seemed as though angels were constantly protecting me, but selfishly, I always needed one or two more favours. I needed help in understanding where this bag had disappeared to, but even more importantly, I needed the good Lord to keep Pauline's mum alive until I had the chance to say my goodbyes. I would never have forgiven myself if I didn't make it before her final departure, so clapping my two hands together, I began to pray deeply.

I contemplated phoning Darnel and telling him, just like his house, my house had been raided but the police had found nothing as the bag had already gone missing, or I thought to myself, would it be better to just run downstairs to where I knew my mum would be sitting and tell her the whole truth and nothing but the truth? I honestly wanted to do the second option and speak to my mum, but I was so caught up, I felt like it would be too much for her to take in. Looking back now, I wish I had spoken to my mum a long time ago, yeah, I know she would have been angry, disappointed most definitely, but at the same time, I knew she would have straightened me out before I was in too deep. Believe me when I say, there's no love like a mother's love.

Dragging my heavy body up, I began the tedious search, tidying up the mess them bloody cops made along the way. I looked under my bed behind my long large mirror in my wardrobe and then in all my draws. I must have looked for hours. I was so hungry by then, it was unreal, but yet I continued, scared that if I stopped, I'd have to face the harsh reality.

Sitting back down, I wondered and reminisced about the good old days, the days when I used to smile a lot, those earlier years when I didn't have a care in the world, it was me just being me. Nowadays, I constantly had a headache or felt jumpy as hell, this wasn't me, this wasn't meant to be my portion, this place felt dark and scary. I was tired of feeling lonely, Darnel had told me from the jump when it came to certain things like our personal life or his belongings, I had to hold information down. I didn't mind at first, but now, so many things had happened it felt as though I was carrying such a heavy burden all alone.

It must have been about midnight before I decided I had to give in to my serious hunger. I was starving and pregnant which was unfair to my child. I only hoped my mum would have gone to bed as she had to be up early for the market with my cousin in the morning. Tomorrow was a new day, the day I would have to pluck up the courage and tell my mum everything.

Walking into the kitchen, I stopped dead in my tracks, my mum was sitting smoking a cigarette in the kitchen with the light off, startling me. "Mum," I stammered as I turned on the kitchen light, frightened that the time had come sooner than I thought to confess all my hidden secrets. "Mum, I have something to tell you," I slowly began, my body temperature rapidly rising, my eyes not blinking.

I was so hungry, I wished my mum had gone to bed, but seeing her sitting there smoking a cigarette, something I had never seen before, made me very nervous. I knew I needed to give her an explanation as to why her house had been raided, there was no getting around this one, but seriously, I only wished I had a little more time so I could at least eat.

My mum stared at me, waiting to hear my explanation. I looked back completely unsure if I should really tell the truth and nothing but the truth. "Mum, I don't where to start but I have something to tell you which I know you're not gonna like, I already know you're gonna be angry with me, but before I start, I just want you to know I'm truly SORRY."

My mum sat in total silence just looking at me, "Mum, I know you raised me well and that's what makes this so hard, but I'm in trouble and I don't know what to do." At that point, I was expecting my mum to interrupt and say something, but she just continued listening.

"There are a few things I'm not very proud of," I confessed, speaking low, playing nervously with my fingers. Taking a deep breath, I continued, "I've been hiding things in the house occasionally for my friend." I looked back up from my fingers and dead in my mum's eyes trying to suss out some sort of reaction, but still, she remained quiet and emotionless.

"The thing is, the stuff I hid in my bedroom for my friend is illegal and dangerous, but somehow, it seems to have vanished, and I don't know what to do." My mum just looked at me, disgusted. I looked back wanting my mum to say something, anything, shout at me, swear at me, slap me even because as crazy as it sounds, the silence was truly deafening me. "So, what was in the bag, Vanessa?" my mum asked, fighting back her tears. I shifted in my seat and then swallowed a huge gulp of air, it was only then that I revealed I couldn't remember exactly what was in the bag, but it was something along the lines of drugs, a gun, bullets and money.

My mum's shoulders flopped forward, her head sank into the palms of her hands, I'd truly done it this time, I'd fully broken her heart. My hunger vanished instantly. How could I think about eating at a time like this? I didn't know what to say to help ease her pain other than, "I'm so SORRY, mum, please forgive me."

I was so numb; I couldn't even cry if I wanted to. I was completely riddled with guilt, I sat there thinking about the times when I was younger and I'd fallen over on my roller-skates and grazed my knee, who was always there to dust me off and let me know everything was going to be ok? Nobody other than this beloved woman herself.

My mum looked up at me full of hurt and, for the second time, spoke, asking me one word, "WHY?" It was pointless to even try and begin to explain because I didn't even fully know why myself. We both sat in silence for a while, deep in thought, then she turned and asked if I had been forced or if I was selling drugs for someone as she knew this couldn't be me. I tried to explain in as little detail as I could that no one had forced me, it had just happened.

"So, how did the police know you were hiding things in my house?" she quizzed, frowning, "None of this makes sense." "I don't know," I replied. "Vanessa, be straight with me; why and who got you into this mess?" I looked away not wanting my mum to read my facial expressions like a book. "It was a boy from school, I didn't do it for a long time, I promise."

"Promise? You f**king promise." My mum shouted, jumping out of her seat as if a spirit had just entered her body. "How dare you bring shit like that into my house, what if Tammy had found the bag and swallowed them drugs? What if she'd picked up the gun and shot herself thinking it was a toy gun? What would you have f**king said to me then? I'm SORRY?" she asked sarcastically.

For the whole time I'd hidden Darnel's stuff, stupidly, not once did any of those two scenarios ever enter my mind, Tammy shooting herself or overdosing on drugs. My mum must have sensed my thoughts because she started screaming louder over and over again, "You never thought about that, did you? I can't believe you've done this to me, I have a good mind to call the police myself." I sat there, frozen, staring at the floor not sure what to say or do next.

"Vanessa, I dunno if you think I'm stupid," my mum barked, slumping back down in the seat she had previously been sitting in, "I know all this has something to do with Darnel." My eyes shot wide open, "Yeah, you think I don't know this has something to do with him, about some boy from your school, there's no boy in your school, is there? Tell me the truth, there's no boy from your school, this is all Darnel's doing."

"I knew there was something I didn't like about him from when you first introduced us, then he goes and gets shot in his arm and you tried telling me it was nothing to do with him, it was wrong place, wrong time. Vanessa, how on earth did you get yourself mixed up with someone like him? I know I don't know the full ins and outs but I'm not silly and this has Darnel written all over it."

"I tell you what you're gonna do," she continued, "you're gonna tell Darnel you're not gonna have anything more to do with him anymore." I looked at her as if to say but I'm pregnant with his baby, but she wasn't caring right now, she was hell-bent on giving me my ultimatum. "So, from now on, you are to have nothing more to do with him or you need to leave my house." I knew she was angry, and I knew I had done wrong, but making me choose, was this really necessary?

"I'm serious, Vanessa, more serious than I've ever been, I don't want somebody like that in yours or my grandchild's life. What if you have a boy and he grows up selling drugs like his dad? What then?" I so wanted to interrupt and say I wouldn't let that happen, but I just looked on and listened. "Seriously, Vanessa, look at me, do you want to take that chance? As you can see, I have done my best by you and look at the situation you're in."

I gazed at my mum, wanting to tell her I was working on him changing his lifestyle, but deep down, I knew she was right, look how many times I had tried subtly talking to him, but he never listened, plus, I had hurt her so badly so I felt I owed this to her. "I know things are not gonna be easy leaving Darnel, but you still have me, I will be by your side as long as you do what's right."

As my mum was getting up, getting ready to leave the kitchen to go to bed, she turned around and said, "oh yeah, by the way, I found that bag you've been looking for all evening a couple of days ago when I was looking for my lip liner, so please tell Darnel I dumped the bag in a bin over in Hackney and if he has a problem with that to come and see me." With that, she walked out of the room, leaving me sitting there, gob smacked.

I sat with a million thoughts threatening to drown my mind. How did my mum find the bag a couple of days ago and not even mention it to me? Would I make it in time to say goodbye to my second mum, Sam? What was I gonna say to my Mr handsome? Imagining Darnel's reaction about not being able to have nothing to do with his unborn baby or losing his bag was my final straw, I didn't know how he was gonna react about any of the two, but regardless of that, my mum had given me an ultimatum and I had chosen her.

Chapter Thirteen

LIFE FOR A DEBT

I awoke with the sickest feeling in my tummy ever. My stomach hadn't stopped hurting me all night. I was on and off the toilet for hours, but still, I was a bit glad to be home alone. My mum had left for the market early in the morning and she'd shipped Tammy out to a family member's house shortly after the raid. I lay there wishing and wanting this peaceful moment to last forever, no headache from anyone, just me on my own. Today was freezing, I could feel the frostbite trying to creep under my covers, if only I could piss off to a beautiful hot tropical island, wouldn't that be great?

I was so engrossed in my wonderful daydreams about walking on a sandy beach with my skin tanning in the hot sun, I barely heard when a text message came through to my phone from Darnel asking me to call him as soon as I woke up. I sat up quick-thinking, OMG what was I gonna tell him? The last time one of his so-called friends called Damien lost the food, he went mad and then remember straight after that he wanted me to knock on that frigging red door.

What would he say? What would he do? No, furthermore, what did he want me to say or do? My mum had found his stash and luckily thrown it away, if she hadn't, I would have been sitting in a police station waiting for court on Monday morning. I bet he wouldn't have come and confessed. If anything, I was the one who should have been upset with him, I begged him to move his stuff and what did he do? Nothing but allow my house to get raided by selling me a shitty dream.

The longer I lay there, the angrier and more frustrated I became, 'Nah, seriously, Vanessa,' I kept on reminding myself, 'if it had been up to him, you seriously wouldn't be sitting in your house right now.' I must've become really brave because the next minute I found myself calling his number. When he answered, I didn't give him a chance, I went for gold letting him know what had taken place the previous day.

I swear I turned into an overnight bad gal cos for a minute or so, I forgot who I was talking to and what he and his soldiers were capable of. He let me ramble on, and then on some more, at the end of my finishing sentence, I let him know my mum had given me an ultimatum and I had chosen her. He remained quiet for a second and then said in the calmest voice ever that he wanted me to meet him ASAP.

I was about to ask him why he wanted to meet but he'd already hung up the phone. My hands began to tremble with anger as I tried to call back his number. I didn't like the fact that he was so calm. Calling him back, I told him in no uncertain terms, I was willing to meet after I'd finished seeing Sam, my second mum.

Wandering around the house before it was time to get myself ready, I couldn't stop myself from crying, all the pressure had become too much.

I had hurt my mum, been given an ultimatum, lost Darnel's bag and needed to say a final goodbye to Sam, Pauline's mum. Nothing seemed to matter right now other than putting everything right, but I just wasn't sure how.

It must have taken me several hours to get ready, deciding on the appropriate clothing to wear, I didn't want anyone to notice I was pregnant, I couldn't handle all the whispering about me being too young to be a mum on top of everything else. I eventually settled on a grey pair of loose jeans with a baggy dark blue jumper and my oversized black new puffer jacket my mum had recently bought me.

When I arrived at the hospital, I was greeted warmly from most of the family and friends that were already there waiting outside in the corridors. I did get one or two stares from friends who were fairly close to Pauline and I, once upon a time. They gave me a look as if they were questioning why I was there. This was neither the time nor the place to bother to even consider their stares. I was here for one purpose and one purpose only, to say my goodbyes.

Walking into the private room filled with more family members with swollen red eyes, my heart completely sank. Sam was hooked up to all kinds of machines, in my opinion, she'd already gone. I squeezed her hand tightly and held it like I never wanted to let it go. The tears began to stream from my eyes, at one point, I thought she gave my hand a little squeeze back to show she knew I was there, but it must have been my hopes or imagination running away with me.

I never moved a muscle until her eldest son asked the people who had already said their goodbyes to leave the room and make way for those outside or just arriving. I gently kissed Sam on her forehead and thanked her for all she had done for me in the past, letting her know I was genuinely thankful. I told her when she was ready, she could leave this world, and one day we would meet again in heaven.

As I was leaving the hospital, I couldn't feel the cold that threatened to bite me this morning. If you had cut me with a knife, I swear I wouldn't have bled. I was like a walking zombie trying to figure out how pain could hurt this much.

Once I had pulled myself together, I called Darnel to arrange to meet as I had still lost all my fear. Initially, I wanted to meet him in a public place just in case he became a little heavy-handed with me, but now, I couldn't care less if he had asked me to meet him in a park after dark. It was as if a small part of me had died as I left the hospital because I felt nothing at all. I just wanted to get this over and done with so I could get on with my life.

Arriving in the McDonald's car park in Green lane a little later on, all my feelings had started to return. I felt somewhat afraid as I pulled the back-door handle of his golf parked waiting on me. "Jump in," he requested in a calm but stern tone, I was starting to slyly regret being a little too brave this morning. "So, Vanessa, tell me again," he begun, "what were you saying to me this morning about my bag going missing and your mum giving you an ultimatum?"

All of a sudden, I heard as he pressed the switch to lock all the doors, my tongue became paralyzed, why on earth did he just lock the doors? I panicked, not once did him or Joseph who was sitting in the front passengers' seat turn around to face me.

"Um..." I began to stutter, "no um," Darnel interrupted, "tell me again what you were saying, trust me, I wanna hear it once more." Again, I began to stutter but then my anger took a hold of me. I felt my Mr Handsome was taking the piss. "I told you already in our earlier conversation that the bag went missing, didn't I? What else do you want me to say?" I asked sarcastically, "My mum found the bag luckily before the police and the BBC turned up and threw the bag away, if anything, you should be pleased," I announced bravely, hoping he would understand.

"So, if your mum found the bag, why didn't she just tell you to give it back to its rightful owner?" "I dunno," I shrugged, "who cares? At least I'm not sitting in a police station or prison cell," by the look he gave me, I wasn't sure if he thought it would've been better if I ended up in one out of the two.

"Are you trying to bump me or something?" he frowned, twisting his face to pure evil, "Cos what you're saying doesn't make any sense to me, no one's mum just finds a bag and throws it away, so who gonna give me back at least the four grand that I've lost?" he turned and looked at me and I looked back at him, pissed he was even asking that question.

"I dunno," I confessed, "you know I don't have any money, so why you asking me?" his stare was starting to freak me out, he turned back around not saying another word and started the engine, "Where we going?" I asked, trying my best not to show I was scared.

Ignoring my question, he repeated himself, "So, who's gonna pay back what I'm owed?" "No-one," I snapped, "no-one is gonna pay back a thing, what do you want me to do? I don't have a penny. Stop the car!" I demanded, vex at him for asking me that silly question twice. He slammed on his brakes and, without warning, turned around and put his two hands around my throat and started to squeeze hard.

"Stop!" I tried to say but it was hopeless, I was struggling to breathe, I was gasping for air, my whole body started flying around frantically trying to get him to release his grip. The more my body resisted him, the tighter the grip became. I thought I was gonna die right in the back of his stupid car. Joseph must've realised he'd been holding my neck for too long and wrestled him to stop.

I wanted to scream out to anybody walking by to help me, but I couldn't, I was coughing non-stop. I tried to open the door to escape his evil pounce but it was no use, the door wouldn't budge. I couldn't believe he had tried to strangle me. "So, Vanessa, tell me again, who's gonna pay back at least the four grand I'm owed?" This time, it was me that snapped, I began trying to punch and scratch him as hard as I could.

How dare he put his hands around my throat. Although I was scared, he had gone too far, today had been such an emotional day for me, saying goodbye to someone I loved. If anything, he should have been holding me tight, letting me know everything was gonna be alright, but instead, he had just strangled me.

He turned around stunned that I had lashed out at him, by now, I was crying inconsolably. "I f**king had to say goodbye to my second mum," I screamed out at him. "So, what did you want me to do, end up in jail?" I screeched, "Huh? Tell me, now you answer me, did you really want me to end up in jail? I told you to move your shit, but you never did and now my mum found it and chucked it away somewhere, and it's my fault."

"Do you truly think I could even try and bump you, Darnel? Do you really think that of me?" I asked, shaking my head in disbelief. He looked back at me with sorrow. I knew he didn't genuinely believe I was that sort of girl that would or could bump him, but I think he had a reputation to protect which seemed to outweigh his feeling towards me.

"Listen," he said half-heartedly, "somehow or someway, you're gonna need to pay back my money." How? I wondered, looking at him confused, "You're gonna need to ask your family or a friend if they have any money they can give you, and oh yeah," he turned around and grabbed my puffer jacket, twisting it tightly in his fingers, pulling me closer to his face. "Let me tell you something from now, don't ever let me hear you say I'm not allowed to have anything to do with my baby, you or your mum must be going mad."

As he let go, he pushed me a little harshly back into my seat. I so wanted to tell him he wasn't gonna have anything to do with this baby or me ever again, especially after today, but I stayed quiet. I couldn't handle a repeat happening all over again. "So, are we clear? You need to find back my money, do you know how much them stuff that was in the bag cost? Do you?" he asked again, punching his fist hard on the dashboard. "Listen, I need to go and sort out the shit you messed up, but I will call you later and we can finish this off then."

He unlocked the car door and I stepped out, grateful to have my feet stood firmly on the ground. I wasn't sure if he had some sort of mental health problems or not, but why did he think he could call me later after what he'd just did? But then again, he could have done much worse to me. So maybe, after all, it was better if I still spoke to him to keep him sweet as I didn't really have a choice.

My mum didn't have to know I still spoke to him, I could just pretend, well, at least for now. I also needed to keep my Mr Handsome cool, if only until I figured out a way to pay him back or convince him otherwise. No way did I ever wanna go through something like that again in my life. A part of me hated him for what he had just done, but the other silly part of my heart made excuses to understand where he was coming from, either way though, through our baby or the money I owed him, I felt indebted to him for life.

Chapter Fourteen

UNTHINKABLE

Coat on and trainers by the front door, yep, nearly ready, now where did I leave my handbag with my money, keys and phone? Opening the kitchen door, I saw my bag sitting on top of the new washing machine! Thank God my mum wasn't in to see where I had left my bag, she would have had a fit. While grabbing my bag to hurry down to the awaiting cab, my phone began to ring.

"Nazarene, I'm on my way, the cab is outside," I said abruptly before she had the chance to moan about me taking too long. "Ok, hurry up!" she replied with a sigh, "The Chinese food my mum ordered for us has arrived and is starting to get cold," "Ok, I said I'm on my way," rushing to put my trainers on, my phone rang again. Really! Did Nazarene not hear me the first time? Why was she ringing me back? Looking at the screen, I saw the name Darnel flashing up, my face broke out into a cheeky grin; I hadn't spoken to him all day.

"Hello, handsome," I answered, still grinning. "Vanessa, I need you to come and meet me now! Bring the bag I left at yours, hurry up, yeah?" "but, Darnel, I'm leaving to go to Nazarene's house," I said a little agitated, not even a 'hi, babes'. "Vanessa!" he said sharply, "did you hear what I said? Come meet me now, it's an emergency. Meet me in Crouch End near where the Cricket club is, make sure the cab drops you off on the main road and then walk up the path and meet me, yeah; make sure the cab doesn't drive up in the alley and remember to bring the black bag with you."

"Sure," was all I could murmur, putting down the phone, once again, I let out a huge sigh. Since that situation last week when he strangled me till I nearly blacked out, things have been slightly different. He'd apologized several times and told me he was being dumb and that he didn't expect me to pay back the four grand, so I tried to get things back to normal.

He even went as far as to ask me after the raid to hold another bag just for a short time, which I did, but now once again I'd had enough of Darnel playing with my emotions, picking me up, making me feel that I was all that mattered in his world, and then other times like now, I feel like shit. How dare this punk not call me all day, especially after the amazing night we'd had, and now call me out of the blue and just expect me to drop what I was doing. I was furious, when was I going to let him know things had to change? If I was busy in the future, then I was just busy.

I ran back up the stairs, two at a time, as quick as I could. I rummaged behind the back of my bed to find Darnel's bag. I ran out to the waiting cab. "Where to, love?" the friendly bald cab driver asked, "Umm, Crouch End," I replied to the unwelcome distraction as my mind wandered back to the repetition of the conversation I just had. "No problem, love, I'll get you there in a jiffy and that will be eight pounds."

Sitting in silence, I now had a few minutes to think about why Darnel wanted me to meet him in such a random place such as the cricket club; what was he up to? Why would he want me to meet him there? Arriving at the meeting spot a few minutes later, I began to feel uneasy, this place was dark, real dark, the floor was littered with dried up fallen leaves. The strong smell of urine hit as if an omen, and to top it all off, rain began to fall, blurring my sight.

Starting the short journey slowly through the alley, I could barely see. With every step I took, I could hear the crunching of leaves beneath my feet. Digging around in my bag for my phone whilst taking pigeon steps, this uneasy feeling was intensifying, suddenly, out of the darkness, I felt a large hand grab me on my shoulder. Spinning around about to scream at the top of my lungs, I saw my Mr handsome standing there.

"Pass the bag," was the order I heard. "Darnel! F**k, man, you scared me, why are you here and why did you want me to meet you here?" "Go to the car," he commanded, "it's parked on the main road and wait for me there." His tone was abrupt, cold. "I won't be that long."

"Help, help," I heard a faint voice call out, stunned at what I had just heard, I looked straight at Darnel who repeated himself. "Go to the car, I'm coming." Ignoring his request, I took a few awkward steps forward towards the faint voice. About 25 feet ahead of us, I sighted Darnel's friends, Joseph and another one called Scott who had recently come out of prison, both stood over a young man kneeling on his knees with his hands tied behind his back, wearing only his orange and white striped boxing shorts for clothing.

The young man looked like he had gone a few rounds with Mike Tyson. Shocked by what I was witnessing, the penny finally dropped. He had asked me here with something in this bag to hurt this guy. "Darnel, Darnel, what the hell are you doing? What's going on here?" I frantically questioned. Roughly yanking my arm to prevent me going any further, he whispered through clenched teeth, "I'm not going to tell you again, wait for me in the car."

Again, I heard the faint voice, "I'm sorry, blood, I'm sorry. Somebody, please help me, fam, shit, I'm sorry, you don't have to do this! It was a mistake, I'm sorry." I could feel his anguish. Scott struck the young man across the head with such force, blood was squirting everywhere. Wait, wait, I tilted my head to the side, I swear I recognised that high-pitch girly voice, I thought to myself. Stepping closer, then closer, Darnel began to grab my coat to try and stop me. Freeing from his grip, approaching the group, I nearly fainted. The young man who had been stripped to his boxers on a freezing cold night, who had clearly been beaten severely, who was barely unrecognisable, was my older brother, Johnathon!

My world completely froze, this was a real-life nightmare I had been lured into. A couple of months earlier, Darnel had been over the moon that one of his closest friends from primary school, Scott, was landing soon from jail. Joseph and Darnel frequently spoke about how mad the roads were gonna be when they all linked back up. When Scott finally came out, I went with Darnel to pick him up from prison, but there was just something about his demeanour that I found to be deadly.

As he jumped in the back of the motor, he went absolutely crazy about a man he had become close to in jail, but the guy had been released about eight or so weeks earlier and was now violating him differently. He didn't go into much detail I believe because I was in the car, but I knew whatever this guy had done to him had to be serious, and by the looks of it, he wasn't gonna let it go.

Soon after Scott's release, I overheard Joseph and Darnel discussing the fact that the guy from jail named Milk, who Scott had become close with inside, was now sleeping with one of his people.

The vibration now coming from my pocket startled me and brought me crashing back to reality. Not now, Nazarene, not now. "Leave him," I wailed at the top of my frantic voice, my steps quickening to protect my older brother. The three of them must have thought I was insane because for a few moments, they all looked completely dumbfounded.

Standing over my almost naked, battered and bruised older brother, I ordered the guys to leave him alone. The response that came out of Scott's mouth still haunts me to this day. "Move, Vanessa, I'm not playing," I stood firmly. "Leave him alone," I yelled again. "He's my brother, do you think I'm gonna stand here and watch you hurt or kill him?" "Your brother, yeah? Your brother, yeah?" Scott said, frothing from the mouth, shuffling closer and closer with the most demonic look, piercing straight through my soul. It was then that I noticed the most seriously menacing, glistening samurai sword you have ever seen held tightly in his hand.

"You know what this cunt has done? You really wanna know what this cunt's done?" he said, raising the sword high above the back of his head. "He's f**ked my mum for f**k sake and given her H.I.V," there was a deafening pause. My mouth flew open, my eyes widened with complete sorrow. How did my older brother manage to sleep with Scott's mum? That was an unspoken rule, a line you just didn't cross, everybody knew that! Surely they did, why would Johnathon sleep with Scott's mum? Darnel and his crew were rated by nuff but hated by most; people feared this group tremendously. I swallowed hard, what had Johnathon done?

I hadn't laid eyes on my brother of whom we shared the same father for the past nine years. He was ten and I was seven when we last saw each other. Johnathon had started to give his mother problems, backchatting, bunking off school, and smoking. So, his mum thinking she was doing the right thing, sent him to live with her Irish twin brothers somewhere abroad.

No matter what though, Johnathon was my older half-brother. I couldn't allow them to kill him. How could I? He was my father's son, what would I say to my dad... 'umm, so sorry, dad, the father of my unborn child and his friends killed your son while I watched!' My family would hate me forever, this situation would tear us apart.

Likewise, to Scott, what did I really think I could say to him right now? 'Umm, so sorry, Scott, my brother shouldn't have been such an arsehole and slept with your mum, giving her H.I.V.' I was in a totally impossible situation here. I wish I could have turned back time to half an hour earlier where I would have been at Nazarene's house eating some tasty food. No, you know what, I wish I could turn back time to six months earlier before I even met Darnel.

Everything changed since meeting him. I've seen things a young girl should never see, been in situations I didn't like, been pulled over by the police with his possessions on me, held his drugs money and guns numerous times. Loved him deeply, got stress from different females, disappointed my mum, was becoming a mum myself aged only 16, and all for what? I stared deep into Darnel's eyes, searching for any type of flicker of help. I closed my eyes, refusing to move away from Johnathon, cradling my four-month unborn child, and waited for the unthinkable pain this sword would cause me. My destiny, my fate, it had come all too soon. I was only 16 with my whole life ahead of me, but I guess that's the price you pay when you get caught in a G's web.

ORGANISATIONS

Vanessa Fox story is fiction inspired by one or two true events, if ever you find yourself in a similar situation, I have given you some organisations that may be able to help you.

Onesimus Services CIC

Onesimus.uk@gmail.com

Telephone 07368-449-808

Onesimus Services with the ELPD Programme (Equipping Lives Pursuing Destiny) A Coaching, Mentoring & Counselling Service.

Aspire 2 Aspire

info@aspire2inspiretraining.org

Aspire 2 Aspire Training An Employability, Mentoring and Coaching Service for parents and young people.

Womanhood Academy

thewomanhoodacademyforgirls@gmail.com

The Womanhood Academy is a powerful Rites of Passage Programme designed to help young girls Transition from Girlhood into Womanhood.

The Manhood Academy

www.manhoodacademy.co.uk

Manhood Academy is a Community-Based Company with a Global Reach that are committed to Life-Changing Transformation opportunities for the Children of our society.

Race Equality Foundation

www.raceequalityfoundation.org.uk

0207-428-1885

Race Equality Foundation work on Safeguarding, Adoption, and Family Support through their projects. Including the evidence based SFSC programme.

COMING *Soon*